Night FIRES

a novel by
GEORGE EDWARD STANLEY

D0967770

Aladdin
NEW YORK LONDON TORONTO SYDNEY

ALADDIN

An imprint of Simon & Schuster Children's Publishing Division
1230 Avenue of the Americas, New York, NY 10020
First Aladdin paperback edition January 2011
Copyright © 2009 by George Edward Stanley
All rights reserved, including the right of reproduction in whole or in part in any form.
ALADDIN is a trademark of Simon & Schuster, Inc., and related logo
is a registered trademark of Simon & Schuster, Inc.
Also available in an Aladdin hardcover edition.
For information about special discounts for bulk purchases, please contact
Simon & Schuster Special Sales at 1-866-506-1949 or business@simonandschuster.com.
The Simon & Schuster Speakers Bureau can bring authors to your live event. For more information or
to book an event contact the Simon & Schuster Speakers Bureau at 1-866-248-3049
or visit our website at www.simonspeakers.com.
Designed by Mike Rosamilia
The text of this book was set in Adobe Caslon Pro.
Manufactured in the United States of America 1110 OFF
2 4 6 8 10 9 7 5 3 1
The Library of Congress has cataloged the hardcover edition as follows:
Stanley, George Edward.
Night fires / by George Edward Stanley.—1st Aladdin ed.
p. cm.
Summary: In 1923, thirteen-year-old Woodrow Harper and his recently widowed mother move
to his father's childhood home in Lawton, Oklahoma, where he is torn between the "right people" of
the Ku Klux Klan and those who encourage him to follow the path of his "nigra-loving" father.
ISBN 978-1-4169-7559-5 (hc)
[1. Race relations—Oklahoma—Fiction. 2. Ku Klux Klan (1915–)—Fiction.
3. Conduct of life—Fiction. 4. Moving, Household—Fiction. 5. Grief—Fiction.
6. Oklahoma—History—20th century—Fiction.] I. Title.
PZ7.S78694Nig 2009
[Fic]—dc22
2008051607
ISBN 978-1-4169-1250-7 (pbk)
ISBN 978-1-4169-9518-0 (eBook)

To Gwen . . .
and to Ellen Krieger
and Susan Cohen

Night Fires is set in an era when America was plagued by ignorance and racism. Verbal abuse and the use of racial epithets were common, as well as the kind of physical brutality described in the novel. There is language in *Night Fires* that should offend and anger, but it accurately depicts the attitudes of some people at the time. It is included to help contemporary readers understand how important it is for our society to overcome these prejudices.

chapter ONE

W here *is* that nigra porter when you need him?"

A well-dressed elderly lady who reminded me of our next-door neighbor back in Washington, D.C., was trying to pull a huge suitcase down the aisle of our day coach.

"Why don't you help her, Woodrow?" Mama whispered to me. "I think this train only has the one porter, and that poor man can't possibly take care of all of the luggage."

"All right, Mama," I said, standing up. This was the first time she had said much of anything since St. Louis. I had been worried about her ever since Daddy died, and I had been hoping this trip would help get her out of her depression. "Ma'am, I'd be happy to carry that for you," I told the woman.

"Well, this poor old widow lady could sure use the help, young man. Thank you." She moved away from the suitcase. "I'm Mrs. Potter. My husband, God rest his soul, was killed in the Great War in 1918, and I've had to manage for myself going on five years now, but as you can see, there are some things I just can't do."

"I'm pleased to meet you, Mrs. Potter, but I'm sorry to hear about your husband, ma'am. I'm Woodrow Harper."

As I picked up the suitcase, which felt as if it were full of bricks, Mrs. Potter whispered, "You pay nigras to do a job, and this is what you get." I thought about what Mama had said about the porter, but I just smiled and let Mrs. Potter lead the way toward the end of our coach. "My sister and her husband are meeting me at the station in Lawton, Woodrow. We're driving to a wedding over in Altus, and I need to be the first one off the train or we'll never make it."

"I'm sorry we're running late, ma'am."

"It's not your fault, Woodrow."

"Well, it is, sort of." We had reached the end of the coach and were standing at the platform door. "We were on the train from Washington, and they delayed this train in Oklahoma City until we arrived."

"Oh," Mrs. Potter said, wrinkling her nose. "You and your folks from up North?"

"It's just my mother and me now. My father was killed in an—"

"We're slowing down, Woodrow!" Mrs. Potter interrupted. She pressed her face against the small window of the platform door. "I'll be mighty displeased if my sister and her husband aren't here waiting for me."

I don't know why I'd thought Mrs. Potter would be interested in hearing the story of my life. For some reason, ever since Daddy died, I'd felt the need to talk to *somebody* about everything that was happening to me—and most of the time Mama didn't seem to be listening anymore. I took a deep breath and let it out, knowing that Mrs. Potter wouldn't hear my frustration over the noise of the train.

Not for the first time since we left, I wished we'd stayed in Washington. I was just starting to make friends there, something that had always been hard for me to do. We moved around so much because of the army. My father, Lt. Col. John Harper, had grown up at Fort Sill, just north of Lawton, where my grandfather had been a cavalry officer. He and Mama had even lived at Fort Sill for a few years when Daddy received his first posting there after graduating from West Point. I had been to Lawton only once, for Grandmother Harper's funeral ten years earlier when I was three. I didn't really remember anything about it, and now we were going to be living there.

"I see them! I see them!" Mrs. Potter shouted, jolting me out of my thoughts. "Now, when the train stops, Woodrow, I want you to open this door and carefully set my suitcase down on the platform. My brother-in-law can carry it from there."

"Excuse me, please." The porter, a large suitcase in each hand, was trying to get past us.

I stepped back, but Mrs. Potter stayed where she was. "You're not putting those suitcases ahead of mine, boy," she said angrily. "I had to carry this heavy thing all the way down the aisle, and I'm not giving up my place to anybody."

"Ma'am, I'll make sure your suitcase is off first, but I have to be the one to open the door," the porter said calmly. "It's the policy of the railroad. Passengers aren't allowed to do that."

The train had stopped, and the other passengers in our coach had formed a line in the aisle while they waited to get off.

Mrs. Potter gave the porter a steely stare, but she moved back, muttering, "There's nothing worse than an uppity nigra."

I saw the porter's mouth twitch, but it remained closed in a grim line. He opened the door and easily swung himself out onto the platform. He offered Mrs. Potter his hand, but she refused it and slipped when she reached the last step. She grabbed hold of the railing, but for a few seconds her feet dangled just above the stool. Finally, Mrs. Potter regained her balance—and her dignity—and stepped onto the platform.

"Mildred!" a woman's voice shouted. Soon a man and woman reached her. The woman looked like a younger version of Mrs. Potter. This had to be her sister and brother-in-law.

"Why didn't you help that lady down?" the brother-in-law demanded of the porter. "She almost fell!"

"I'm all right," Mrs. Potter said huffily. "I'm all right."

Mrs. Potter's sister stared at the porter and mumbled, "What is this world coming to?"

The brother-in-law picked up the suitcase, and the three of them headed away from the train. As they walked off, I heard him say, "That's why I'm so proud of what the Klan is doing in this state. They're going to put a stop to the way these nigras have started treating white people."

I stood back, letting the rest of the passengers get off the train, before going back to our seats to help Mama with the luggage. But I couldn't stop looking at the porter. I could tell by his eyes that he was upset by more than the rudeness of Mrs. Potter and her family.

Mama was still sitting, staring out the window, when I got to our seats. I began taking our belongings from the overhead rack. We had only two small suitcases with the things we'd needed in our Pullman compartment; we had shipped everything else by American Railway Express. Mama stood up slowly and followed me back down the aisle. The porter was still at the coach door. He took our suitcases and set them down onto the platform. Mama said, "Thank you," and the porter replied, "Yes, ma'am," politely but absentmindedly.

Mama and I picked up our suitcases and headed down the platform. Several soldiers passed us walking in semiformation toward an old bus that would take them out to Fort Sill. I was shocked when one of them winked at Mama. Her face turned bright red, and I knew if Daddy were still alive, he would have lit into that soldier. Was *I* supposed to do that now? The thought gave me a knot in my stomach, so I decided to pretend I hadn't seen it happen.

As we passed the colored-only waiting room, four Negro soldiers almost collided with us as they ran out to catch up with the white soldiers. Mama's friend Winifred Renfro, who taught English at Lawton High School, had said she would meet us, but she wasn't in the whites-only waiting room, so Mama and I sat down on one of the wooden benches. "I'll be glad when we get to the house, Woodrow," she said with a deep sigh. "I am so very tired."

"I'll be glad too, Mama." I stood up. "I need to go to the men's room." When I got there, it was full of cigarette smoke, and I had to maneuver around several soldiers standing in little groups.

"Can you believe this place?" one said as he dried his hands.

"It's worse than Kansas," said another one, "and I thought that was the end of the world."

"Hey, we need to get on the bus," a third solider said, grinding the butt of his cigarette into the floor with the heel of his boot.

They all hurried out, leaving me alone with the smell and the silence.

Winifred and Mama were standing together talking when I left the men's room. Mama turned my way just as I reached them. "I was getting worried about you."

"I'm okay. Hello, Winifred!"

"Hello, Woodrow. It's so good to see you again. You're even taller than when I last saw you—at your daddy's funeral." She eyed me up and down. "Peggy, he's the spittin' image of John."

"Yes, he is, isn't he?" Mama said with a tired smile. She took a deep breath. "Woodrow and I are exhausted, Winifred," she added. "Can we continue this conversation at the house?"

"Of course! My car's out this way," Winifred said. "I can hardly wait for you to see it," she added, a big grin spreading on her face. "Come on!" She led us out of the waiting room. "I'm glad that some Harpers are finally moving back into the Harper house. It just seems right."

Daddy had known Winifred before he and Mama got married, and she and Mama had been friends ever since Daddy was stationed at Fort Sill. Winifred had even come to Washington for Daddy's funeral. Right before she boarded the train for the trip back, she'd said, "There's no reason for you and Woodrow to stay up here, Peggy. You should move to Lawton and live in the Harper house. I can even help you get a teaching job at Lawton High School."

Mama's parents were dead, and she wasn't close to the few cousins she had in nearby Maryland, so by the time Winifred got back to Oklahoma, Mama had made up her mind. She'd do what Winifred had suggested. Once during the trip Mama said, "This was what your daddy dreamed of doing, Woodrow: returning to Lawton after he retired. He had some wonderful memories of growing up at Fort Sill. He wanted you to have those same memories." Why hadn't I known that? It seemed like it wasn't until after he died that I realized how little time my father and I had had to talk to each other. I was hoping the move to Lawton would help me get to know him better.

There was only one automobile in the gravel parking lot, so it had to be Winifred's. "Well, what do you think?" she asked.

"It's lovely," Mama said.

I was really impressed too. "It's a 1922 Lafayette, four-door touring car," Winifred said proudly. "James bought it in Oklahoma City last week. It's an anniversary present." She laughed. "Of course, he drives it mostly. You know how husbands can be. It's too bad we live only one block from the high school, because I don't really have a good excuse to drive it there."

I put our suitcases on the backseat and got in beside them. As we headed down E Avenue, Mama said, "Oh, my goodness, Winifred. What is that all about?"

The suitcases were blocking my view out Mama's window, so I leaned forward. She was watching two people walk down the sidewalk. They were dressed in white robes with white hoods over their faces. "There have been a few changes since you were here last," Winifred said slowly. "The Ku Klux Klan is now firmly established in Lawton."

Mama gasped. "You can't be serious." She had an anxious look on her face. "Why, for goodness' sakes?"

I remembered what Mrs. Potter's brother-in-law had said about the "Klan."

"Oh, don't worry about it, Peggy. The Klan here isn't like the Klan down South. They're not out to bother the Negroes or the Jews or the Catholics." Winifred laughed. "We don't have many of those, anyway."

"Well, then, why *are* they here?" Mama asked.

"Lawton can be a bit rough. In many ways, it's still like the Old West. The Klan is helping us clean things up, and frankly, I'm glad they're here. There are a lot of us who think the Klan can make this a better place to live."

"Well, I don't know how I feel about that, Winifred. It's quite a shock seeing them on the streets like this. I thought they did everything in secret."

Winifred shrugged. Just as she turned a corner, though, she looked over at Mama and said, "From what I hear, the members of the Klan are all good Christian people, Peggy." As she pulled into the driveway of a large two-story white-frame house, she added, "But James and I have decided it's better not to talk too much about it. And, as your friend, that's what I'm advising you to do."

chapter TWO

Mama leaned toward the windshield. "Oh, Winifred! I had honestly forgotten how lovely this house was!"

"It's always been one of the showplaces in Lawton, Peggy, and it hasn't changed at all since Mrs. Harper died."

"I'm glad to hear that," Mama said.

"James and I were able to get Eloise Johnson, one of the Domestic Science teachers at Cameron State School of Agriculture, to live here. Mrs. Harper's colored woman, Jenny, stayed on to keep house for her. When Jenny died last year, her daughter, Mary, took over."

"Was Miss Johnson upset at having to move out?" Mama asked.

"Oh, goodness, no, Peggy, this house was always too big for her. Her family was friends with the Harpers, and Eloise just considered herself a caretaker. Instead of paying rent, she paid Jenny and Mary's salaries, and that worked out just fine for everyone concerned."

I was looking around as Mama and Winifred spoke. "Who lives next door?" I asked. "I've never seen such a gorgeous garden." I'd always loved flowers.

"That's Senator Crawford's house," Winifred replied.

"Senator Crawford?" Mama asked.

"Oh, yes, George Crawford is your neighbor." Winifred nodded to the house on the right. "He's a member of the Oklahoma legislature—and a widower. His son, Robert, was killed in France during the war, and his wife passed on not too long after that. When I told George about you and Woodrow moving in here, he said to be sure and let him know if you ever need anything. It can be hard getting around here without a car." Winifred sighed. "He's such a lonely man." Mama raised an eyebrow and gave Winifred a hard stare. Winifred returned it. "Peggy! He's at least fifteen years older than you, for goodness' sake!" In a lower voice, she added, "Although that's not always so bad."

"I plan to buy an automobile as soon as I can, Winifred. I wouldn't want to impose on the senator."

We had a new Essex when we lived in Washington, but Daddy was driving it when he was killed, and Mama said she never wanted to see it again.

"Come on," Winifred said. "Let's go inside. I'm sure Mary has everything spic-and-span."

I counted ten wooden steps up to the front porch. When I reached the top, I turned and looked back down at the street. I was surprised at how far I could see.

Winifred opened the front door, and we stepped into a large foyer divided by a wide staircase. This house was bigger than any house we had ever lived in.

"Oh, Winifred, it's just as I remember!" Mama said.

I noticed the delicious scent of fresh-baked bread. Winifred sniffed the air at the same time. "I forgot to tell you that Mary is a wonderful cook too."

"She sounds perfect," Mama said.

"I was so glad you decided to keep her on, Peggy. She really needs this job. She's trying to keep her son in school, but he can't seem to stay out of trouble. And that lazy good-for-nothing husband of hers is gone most of the time and drunk when he's around. Anyway, you couldn't find better help."

Just then a Negro woman came out of the kitchen drying her hands on a tea towel. She had a big smile on her face, but when she got closer, her eyes looked sad, and I could tell she had been crying. "I'm sorry, Mrs. Renfro. I heard the door, but I was, uh, taking some bread out of the oven, so I just, uh . . ." She looked at Mama. "Are you Mrs. Harper?"

"Yes, I'm Peggy Harper, and this is my son, Woodrow. Mrs. Renfro has been singing your praises, Mary. We're delighted that you've agreed to stay on."

"Thank you so much, Mrs. Harper. I'm very happy here, and I can make any changes you want in the way I keep house or in the way I cook."

"Oh, let's not worry about that . . ." Mama stopped. A Negro boy about my age had appeared in the doorway behind Mary.

Winifred gasped. "Mary! What is Joshua doing here?" she demanded. "You know what I've told you about that."

Mary's smile disappeared, and now her face matched her eyes. "I know what you said, Mrs. Renfro, and I know what I promised, but Joshua here—"

"It's all right," Mama said, interrupting her. "We can discuss this later. Woodrow, why don't you and Joshua look around the rest of the house?" She turned to Mary. "We could certainly use a cup of coffee, if you'd brew some, couldn't we, Winifred?"

Winifred nodded.

"I'll bring it to you ladies in the parlor," Mary said. "It's right this—"

"No, no, we'll join you in the kitchen, Mary," Mama said. "That'll give us a chance to talk some more about your duties."

Joshua hadn't moved. As Mary headed back to the kitchen with Mama and Winifred, she said, "You heard Mrs. Harper, Joshua. It's all right for you to look around the house with Mr. Woodrow."

Joshua stepped aside to let Mama, Winifred, and his mother pass, and then he started walking slowly in my direction, not once taking his eyes off me. I swallowed hard. From the look on his face, he was really angry about something, but I made a point of meeting his stare. When he reached me, I held out my hand and said, "Woodrow Harper." For just a moment, I was sure Joshua wasn't going to shake it, but he finally did, and it struck me that I had never touched a Negro before. "Where do you want to go first?" I asked.

Joshua shrugged. "I don't know. I've never seen anything except the kitchen. I always knock on the back door, and my mama lets me in, and I stay in there until it's time to leave."

"Then let's just do it room by room," I suggested. It turned out I mostly looked around the upstairs by myself. Joshua was always a few steps behind, and after a while I got tired of stopping and waiting for him. Finally, I'd had enough. "What are you so angry about?" I asked him.

The question took him by surprise. "Nothing," he said sullenly.

"I'm just trying to be friendly, Joshua."

"Nobody asked you to be friendly to me. I came here to see my mama, because I had something I needed to talk to her about."

"What?"

"It's none of your concern."

I stared at him for a couple of minutes, but when he didn't even blink, I finally said, "You're right, it's none of my concern."

I started to leave the room, but Joshua didn't move, so I stopped too. My reply must have taken him by surprise. "Why do you want to live in this town?" he asked.

"Mama has a teaching job at the high school. We were planning to move back here anyway when my father retired from the army, because he grew up on Fort Sill, but he was killed a few months ago in a car accident."

I sort of expected Joshua to say something like "I'm sorry

about that," but he didn't. Instead he said, "Well, there's no way I'm staying here. I'm taking a freight train up to Chicago. I've got an uncle there who says he'll put me up and help me find a job. There's lots of jobs for colored folks in Chicago."

"What about school?" I asked.

Joshua snorted. "What do I need school for? I already know what I need to know. I can tell you where every freight train leaving Lawton is going and what time it'll get there."

"Daddy wanted me to go to West Point so I could become an officer like he was." When Joshua didn't say anything, I added, "But I don't really want to." Joshua just continued to stare at me, making me very uncomfortable. "Let's go back downstairs," I said. But as we left the room, I noticed a pull-down ladder at the end of the hall. "That must be how you get to the attic. Do you want to go see what's up there first?"

Joshua shook his head. "It's probably just full of spiders."

"Let's have a look anyway," I said.

"You go ahead. I don't like spiders."

"Somehow I didn't think you'd be afraid of anything, Joshua."

"I'm not. I just don't like them."

"Okay. I don't have to look up there now. There's plenty of time to do it later."

"If you're thinking I'm too scared to go up there—"

"I'm not thinking anything of the sort, Joshua. I just decided I didn't want to go up there right now."

"You're lying!" Joshua brushed past me. When he reached the ladder, he pulled it down and started climbing. I hurried to the end of the hall and followed him up.

At the top was a narrow landing in front of a door. Joshua tried the handle and the door opened. I had reached his knees and was peering between his legs into the attic. What I saw didn't look too bad. Joshua went inside, and I was right behind him. "There must be a light around here somewhere," I said, though the two windows on either side of the large room let in enough light for us to find our way around.

"Here's a string." Joshua pulled on it and the entire attic was illuminated. It wasn't at all what I expected. It was a little dusty, but it was more like another room in the house than a storage area. "I've never seen an attic like this. I've only been in attics with lots of spiders," Joshua said.

"Me too." I walked over to him. "I don't like spiders either."

The beginning of a grin started on Joshua's mouth, but it was extinguished almost as quickly. He turned away and started walking around. Again I followed. Up against one wall, I saw a rocking horse and a wagon and a sled. Beyond them were two boxes on which someone had written JOHN's TOYS. I felt my heart flutter. "These were Daddy's when he was a boy!"

I opened one of the boxes and saw some wooden horses. I took out a couple and started to hand one to Joshua, but he said, "I've got better things to do than look at little kids' toys." I didn't feel like arguing with him, so I put the two horses back in the box.

In the second box, I found some metal soldiers. I could tell by the uniforms that they were Civil War figures. I wondered if Daddy had spent hours imagining what he himself would do in battle when he became a soldier. I didn't want to think about that, so I closed up the box and walked over to where Joshua was standing by some old leather trunks. On the side of each one, someone had pasted labels and written dates and what was inside. "'John's baby clothes, 1877–1880,'" I read. "That's when Daddy was born, 1877," I told Joshua. "These clothes are forty-five years old."

"They're probably rotten by now," Joshua said.

The trunk wasn't locked, so I undid the hinges and opened the lid. A strong smell burned my nose, causing me to back away.

"Mothballs," Joshua said.

"What?"

"Mothballs! You've never heard of mothballs before?" Joshua picked up a little white ball and smelled it. "It keeps moths from eating the cloth," he added, tossing the ball back into the trunk. "These aren't very old either. Somebody must have put them in recently." He closed the lid and wiped his hands on his pants. "That stuff's poison."

I wondered if this attic, filled with my father's things, would help me understand more about him and what he was like when he was my age. I followed the clothes trunks around the attic.

JOHN'S CLOTHES, 1880–1881.

JOHN'S CLOTHES, 1882–1884.

JOHN'S CLOTHES, 1885–1887.

They stopped at 1896.

I did some calculating in my head. "Daddy was nineteen years old in 1896," I said. "That's the year he went to West Point."

But Joshua wasn't listening to me. I heard a noise, like a grunt, and looked up to see him standing at one of the windows. His fists were tightly clenched. "What's wrong?" I asked.

When he didn't answer, I walked over to see what he was

looking at. There on the sidewalk the next block over were more robed Klansmen. They were slowly walking back and forth in front of one particular house. "Why are they doing that?"

"The woman who cleans for those people has a son named Theodore," Joshua whispered. "He ran away last week, and the Klan is trying to find him."

chapter THREE

"Why?" I asked, but Joshua didn't answer, and we continued to look out the window in silence as the Klansmen paraded back and forth in front of the house. Then a side door opened and a white man hurried out to the sidewalk. He shook hands with the Klansmen and started talking to them. I pressed my nose to the window. The scene below was like one of the movies that Mama and Daddy had sometimes taken me to see at the Biograph in Washington. The man was moving his mouth, but I couldn't hear the words. In the movie, you had to wait until they appeared on the screen. I wished that could happen here. One of the Klansmen pointed to the man's house. The man gestured and moved his mouth up and down and around some more. The Klansmen nodded, and they all shook hands again. The man went back into his house, and the Klansmen walked to a big black car parked down the street and drove off.

When I turned around, Joshua was no longer in the attic. I thought about going downstairs to look for him but decided I was more interested in checking out the things in the trunks than I was in talking about the Klan.

I went back to the old leather trunk labeled 1890, unlatched it, and opened the lid. Once again I was assaulted by the smell of mothballs, so I waited a couple of minutes until some of the stronger fumes had escaped and then began pulling out the contents. There were shirts, knickerbockers, socks, and shoes. I held up a pair of the knickerbockers and could tell they would fit me perfectly. *Daddy was the same size as me when he was my age,* I thought, and that made me feel happier than I had been in weeks. I had a sudden urge to try on the clothes, so I took out a pair of tan knickerbockers, a white shirt with ruffles on the front, some socks that were almost knee-high, and a pair of brown leather shoes. There was also a brown leather belt at the bottom of the trunk, under some more shoes. Everything smelled like mothballs, but I was too intent on changing into Daddy's clothes to be bothered by it.

In the far corner of the attic, I spotted an old mirror propped up against the wall. I walked over and looked at myself. It gave me a funny feeling to think that Daddy had once worn these same clothes. It could have been the fact that the mirror had a layer of dust on it, making me look fuzzy, but for just a minute I felt like I was seeing a ghost.

I thought Mama would be excited about what I had found, so I headed downstairs to the kitchen. When I pushed opened the door, Mary was standing at the stove stirring something in a pot. Mama was sitting at the kitchen table, a coffee cup poised at her lips, listening to what Mary was saying. I suddenly felt a little foolish dressed in those old clothes, so I was glad that Winifred and Joshua weren't there.

"Hello," I said.

Mama turned to me, blinked a couple of times, then stood up. "Oh, Woodrow! You startled me! My goodness! For just a minute there, I thought I was looking at a picture of your father. Where did you find those clothes?"

"In the attic," Mary replied for me. "I don't think old Mrs. Harper would want those clothes disturbed either, Mr. Woodrow," she added.

Mama continued to stare at me. "Where did you find those

clothes, Woodrow?" she asked again. It was obvious she hadn't been listening to what Mary said.

"In the attic," I told her. "There are all these old leather trunks full of Daddy's clothes. Grandmother Harper must have kept everything he ever owned, because the trunks are labeled by years, from when Daddy was born until he went away to West Point."

"Oh, that is so wonderful." It had been a long time since I had seen Mama's eyes so bright, and that made me happy. "I had no idea." She turned to Mary. "Is it true?" There was excitement in her voice.

"Yes, ma'am," Mary said. Suddenly she took a deep breath and looked over at us. "Nobody has ever touched those trunks, Mrs. Harper, except to put new mothballs in each one every year." She went back to stirring the pot. "Mr. John's clothes were very important to old Mrs. Harper, and she wouldn't want people to disturb them."

"I don't think she would have meant us, Mary," Mama said. "I really don't." She took me by the elbow and said, "I want to show you a photograph, Woodrow." I followed Mama into the foyer. She opened one of the suitcases that were pushed up against the wall. Under some of her clothes was a small parcel wrapped in tissue paper. Mama took it out, unwrapped it, and for just a moment held the frame protectively against her chest before she handed it to me. "This is one of my treasures, Woodrow."

It was a picture of a boy who looked exactly like me and who was wearing the clothes I had on now. My heart started to pound. "Is this Daddy?"

Mama nodded. "He was thirteen too, Woodrow, when this was taken. You can imagine why I was so startled when I saw you in these clothes."

We were interrupted by a knock at the front door. Even though Mama and I were just a few feet away, Mary came out of the kitchen, wiping her hands on her apron, and opened it. A man was standing on the porch. Beyond him I saw an old truck parked in front of the house. It was painted dark green and had the words AMERICAN RAILWAY EXPRESS AGENCY on the side. "Hello, Mary," the man said. "I'm delivering Mrs. Harper's trunks."

"Yes, sir, Mr. Wallace. I'll show you where to put them, sir."

"Billy, Bobby, let's get a move on," Mr. Wallace shouted toward the truck.

Two boys who looked a few years older than I jumped out of the cab of the truck, hurried around to the rear, opened the doors, and pulled out one of our trunks, which they carried by the leather end handles as easily as if it were empty. While the man had his back turned, I slipped away to the attic and quickly changed into my regular clothes. When I started back downstairs, Billy and Bobby were heading up. "Why don't you show them where your room is, Woodrow?" Mama said. "That trunk has your clothes in it. The ones with your books and other things will be coming up in a minute."

My room was at the end of the hall. It had been Daddy's.

Billy and Bobby set the trunk down gently on the rug and then left. I opened it and started hanging my clothes in the closet. On the floor beneath them I lined up my shoes in neat rows. Billy and Bobby brought up the other two trunks, and I spent the next couple of hours arranging my room. Once I thought I heard Mama talking with Mary in her bedroom, just down the hall, but I couldn't hear what they were saying. I had just finished putting the last book on the bookshelf when I noticed Mary standing at my door. "What did you do with your daddy's clothes?" she asked.

"I put them back in the trunk in the attic. Why?"

"It's not good to live with the dead, Mr. Woodrow," Mary said in a soft voice. "It's not good at all. I know it's none of my business, but I don't want to happen to your mama what happened to your grandmother Harper after your grandfather

Harper died, so I hope you and your mama will leave the dead alone and live your own lives."

Before I could ask Mary what she meant, she slipped out of my view, and I heard only the sound of her shoes on the hardwood floor of the hallway. But her words made me want to see how Mama was doing, so I walked down the hallway to her bedroom. She was hanging Daddy's clothes in the closet. I hadn't even known she had brought them from Washington. "Why are you doing that?" I asked.

"Because it makes me feel like your father's still here, Woodrow," Mama said as she put one of Daddy's shirts on a hanger. "Mary told me that there was space for them up in the attic, but I'm just not ready to put them away yet." She turned and looked at me. "I'm all right, Woodrow. It's just going to take some time."

I stood there, not knowing how to respond. Finally I said, "If you need anything, just call me, all right?" But Mama no longer seemed to be listening to me.

I suddenly felt as if I had to get out of the house. I stepped onto the front porch and sat in one of the white wicker chairs. The weather was pleasant, although a little hotter than it would have been in Washington, and the fresh air made me feel better. Somewhere in the distance, I thought I heard some boys shouting and laughing.

I looked up as a car pulled into the driveway next door and a man leaned out the window. "Are you Woodrow?" he asked.

I nodded. "Yes, sir."

"Well, I'm pleased to meet you, Woodrow. I'm George Crawford."

Senator Crawford, I remembered. I walked over to the automobile. "I'm very pleased to meet you, Senator Crawford," I said, offering him my hand, which he took and grasped in a tight shake. "Winifred Renfro told Mama and me that you lived here."

Senator Crawford let go of my hand, opened the car door, and stepped out. He was taller than Daddy and a little heavier, but not fat. Right away, I sensed that he was someone very important. "Well, Woodrow," he said, putting a warm hand on my back, "I am really glad to have you and your mother as my neighbors. It's good to have Harpers back in this house again."

"Thank you, sir."

Senator Crawford leaned against his automobile and looked at me. "You make me think of my son, Robert. He was killed in France in the Great War."

"Winifred told us about that. I'm sorry, sir."

"His mother never got over it, and she died not too

long after that. I've been trying to make sense of it ever since." I didn't know what to say. As if he suddenly realized that, Senator Crawford added, "Well, that was no way to greet a new neighbor, and I'm sorry, Woodrow. It's just that, sometimes, when I start thinking about it all, it overwhelms me so."

"You don't have to be sorry, sir. I sometimes start thinking about what happened to my father, and it just sort of, well, overwhelms me too, I guess."

Senator Crawford gave me a big smile and said, "You and I have that in common, then, and I hope we can become friends." He looked at our house. "Is your mama where I could say hello to her?"

"She was hanging up her clothes when I came outside, but I could go …"

"No, don't do that. I won't bother her now." Senator Crawford patted me on the back. "Do you like to fish, Woodrow? Maybe we could go fishing sometime. I miss doing things with my son. Maybe you and I could …" He hesitated. "You're probably busy with your own activities, though, so …"

"Oh, no, I'd like that very much. I've never been fishing before, and I've always wanted to."

"Well, then, I'll talk to your mother about it soon. In fact, maybe the three of us could go to dinner some evening at Medicine Park," Senator Crawford said. "How does that sound?"

I had no idea where Medicine Park was, but I said, "I think it sounds great, sir!"

chapter FOUR

Mama, I just met Senator Crawford, and he said that he wanted to . . ." I stopped in the middle of my sentence. All of a sudden I was back in Mama and Daddy's bedroom in Washington. Everything was arranged exactly as it had been there.

Mama finished hanging a picture of Daddy on the wall, gave me a big smile, and said, "What's this about Senator Crawford, sweetheart?"

"I just met him a few minutes ago, and he said that he wanted to take me fishing one of these days, and he also said that he wanted to come over here sometime and meet you and that he'd really like to take both of us to dinner at Medicine Park."

Mama wrinkled her brow. "Why would he want to do all that?"

"He told me he was happy that some Harpers were back living in this house again. That's what Winifred said too. Remember? I guess that's the reason."

"Well, that's nice, Woodrow, and please thank him for me, but . . ." Her eyes drifted back to the picture of Daddy on the wall. "I'm too tired now even to think about going out to dinner."

"All right, Mama, but he seems really nice, and I'd like to go with . . ." I started to say, but stopped because once again Mama was no longer listening.

As Mama and I started to get settled in Lawton, I realized that when we went out, Mama seemed almost her normal self, but as soon as we returned home, she withdrew into her bedroom, where she was surrounded by Daddy's things. I spent my days trying to think of places for Mama and me to go. Finally I ran out of ideas, and I could no longer stand being inside the house. Except for Mary and Joshua, the only person I'd met in Lawton was Senator Crawford, and I found myself thinking about him.

"Mama, why don't I go tell Senator Crawford that we'd like to have dinner with him at Medicine Park? He said to let him know when we were ready, and I think we're ready, don't you?" That first part wasn't really true, but somehow I didn't think Senator Crawford would care.

"Oh, Woodrow, I don't feel up to socializing yet, and besides, Mary is preparing a nice dinner for us here."

"It's been two weeks, Mama. I want to go!" I surprised myself at how forcefully I had spoken. "I'd really like to go out," I added, this time not quite as strongly.

Mama sighed. "I don't want to go, Woodrow, but if you want to go by yourself, I don't mind."

"Thank you, Mama. I'll go talk to Senator Crawford right now."

I left the room and bounded down the stairs, but on the front porch, I stopped and took a deep breath. I felt guilty about leaving Mama, but I kept thinking about what Mary had said about not living in the past. I wanted to start a new life here in Lawton. I ran across our lawn and up onto Senator Crawford's front porch. I was just about to knock when the door suddenly opened.

"Woodrow!" Senator Crawford said. "How nice to see you!"

"Mama said I could go to dinner with you . . . sometime . . . if you still want to," I said, barely above a whisper. "She's too tired, but . . . I think she'll want to go some other time."

"Well, I certainly hope so." Senator Crawford opened the screen door to let me inside. "I'm sorry I've not yet paid my respects to her, but I've been in Oklahoma City on senate business. As it turns out, though, I am having an early dinner at Medicine Park today, so I'm glad you came over. If you'd like, you may sit in my study while I finish getting ready." At that moment, an old Negro man appeared in the doorway on the other side of the room, startling me. "Have you laid out my clothes, Benjamin?" Senator Crawford asked him.

"Yes, Senator," Benjamin replied.

"This is Woodrow Harper, Benjamin. He and his mother have moved into the Harper house next door. You remember the Harpers, don't you?"

"Yes, sir, Senator, I think I do," Benjamin replied.

Senator Crawford turned to me. "Benjamin's getting a little feeble in mind and body, Woodrow. He's supposed to be taking care of me, but sometimes I think it's the other way around. He's been with me for a long time, Benjamin has. He knows everything there is to know about me." He looked back at Benjamin. "Bring Woodrow some lemonade and show him to my study."

"Yes, sir, Senator," Benjamin said. He turned and disappeared from view, but I heard him opening what I thought were probably cupboard doors, so I knew the kitchen was just beyond where he had been standing.

"Benjamin makes the best lemonade in the world," Senator Crawford said. "His cooking leaves a bit to be desired these days, though, but I don't mind eating at restaurants. It gets me out of the—"

Just then Benjamin reappeared with a small tray and a tall glass of lemonade. "Will you follow me, sir?" he said. It took me a moment to realize that he was talking to me.

"I'll be ready in a few minutes," Senator Crawford said.

I followed Benjamin down a hallway and into Senator Crawford's study. The curtains were drawn, and the furniture was dark, but there was a lamp lit in the corner. Benjamin set the tray with the glass of lemonade down on a small table next to a chair beside a cluttered desk. "If you need anything else, sir, just come to the door and shout for me. I don't hear as well as I used to, so you may have to do it several times."

"All right, Benjamin," I said. "Thank you." I took a long sip of the cold lemonade and thought that Senator Crawford was right. It really was delicious. After a second sip, I began to relax. I felt comfortable in this room. It had books everywhere. There were also some photographs on the desk—in one, Senator Crawford was standing with a woman and a younger man in an army uniform. I was sure they were his wife and his son. Just as I took a third sip of lemonade, I saw the back of an easel in the corner of the room. I stood up and walked over to it. The portrait was only half finished, but I could tell that it was Robert.

"Do you like it?"

The voice startled me. When I looked around, Senator Crawford was standing in the doorway. He had changed into a pair of khaki pants and a light blue short-sleeved shirt. "I'm sorry, sir. I didn't mean to bother your things."

Senator Crawford came into the room. "You're not bothering my things. I wanted you to make yourself at home." He walked over to the easel. "Not many people know that I paint, Woodrow, but now you're one of them."

"I like to draw, but I've never painted like this and I've always wanted to." I hesitated. "In fact, I even think I'd like to be an artist when I grow up."

"Really? That's exactly what I wanted to be when I was your age!"

I hadn't expected that of Senator Crawford, and it was exciting to think I had something in common with such an important person. "I never told anyone before, because Daddy always assumed I'd become an army officer like he was."

"I never told my parents what I really wanted to be either, Woodrow, and sometimes I'm angry with myself that I didn't, because . . . well, that's water under the bridge, as they say. There's no use in trying to undo the past, but we can certainly do something about the present, can't we? We'll just have to do something about your wanting to be an artist."

"Do you mean that?"

"Of course I mean it!" Senator Crawford looked at the unfinished portrait. "At first I tried to paint Robert from some of the pictures I have, but I couldn't get his expression right, so I decided I'd try to recreate him from memory, and that was what I needed to do."

"His face does look real, sir," I said.

"I think so," Senator Crawford said softly. He took a deep breath. "Well, I'm getting hungry. How about you?"

"I am too."

"You'll like Medicine Park. It's a little resort town out in the Wichita Mountains. I'll tell you all about it on the drive out there. Do you like to swim?"

I nodded. "Well, there's a lovely pool at Medicine Park," the senator went on. "I have a pair of Robert's swimming trunks you could use."

I wondered if they would smell of mothballs like Daddy's

old clothes. And how old-fashioned would they be? "I'll just run home and get mine," I said.

Senator Crawford smiled as if he knew what I was thinking. "I couldn't bear to throw away any of his things."

"It'll just take me a minute," I said, hurrying to the front door.

I was hoping I could grab my trunks and get back to Senator Crawford's house without anyone noticing, but I saw Mary watching me intently from the kitchen doorway. For some reason her stare made me uncomfortable.

"Are you all right, Woodrow?" Senator Crawford asked me when I met him in his driveway.

"Yes, sir, I was just thinking about something. This is a really nice automobile, Senator Crawford. What kind is it?"

"It's a 1922 Buick Touring. Isn't she a beauty?"

I nodded. "Mama said we're going to get another automobile soon. We had one in Washington, but Daddy was in it when he was . . ."

"I know it's hard for you, losing your daddy," Senator Crawford said, "and, well, I can . . ." He stopped. "You and I have both suffered terrible losses, Woodrow, and I think we can help each other to understand why things like this happen to good people."

No one had ever told me I could help him understand what had happened to him, and I liked the feeling it gave me. "I wouldn't mind doing that at all."

"Good! Now, let's head out to Medicine Park."

"Do you want me to crank it for you? I used to do that for Mama and Daddy sometimes."

"This model has an electric starter, Woodrow. Of course, it also has a crank, just in case something happens to the starter." He grinned. "I guess these newfangled contraptions don't always work, so it's good to have a backup plan."

"Yes, sir."

"Actually, I think it's good to have a backup plan for everything in your life, Woodrow. You never know when you'll have to make some changes in it."

"I never thought about that before, but it makes sense. You don't think that your father is going to get killed, so when it happens, you have to figure out how you're going to live without him."

Senator Crawford nodded. "We can't seem to get on the road here, can we? But that's a good thing, Woodrow. When you keep talking to someone, when you really should be doing something else, then that just means you and that person have a lot to share with each other."

"I agree, sir."

"But my stomach's beginning to growl, so I think it's telling me that we should continue our sharing over some food."

I laughed. "My stomach's growling too. I think it must be talking to your stomach."

"See! What did I tell you, Woodrow? Our stomachs have already decided they're going to be good friends."

With that we both got into the Buick Touring, and Senator Crawford pushed the electric starter. The automobile shook and came to life. On purpose I didn't glance over at our kitchen window as we backed out of the driveway to see if Mary was looking at me again. I didn't want to think about anything else except being in this automobile with Senator Crawford as we headed toward Medicine Park to eat and to talk about helping each other deal with all the problems in our lives.

chapter FIVE

It wasn't long before we had left Lawton behind and were on a narrow dirt road headed for Medicine Park. "This isn't the shortest route, Woodrow, but it's the most scenic, and this way you'll get to see more of the Wichita Mountains. All of us out around here think they're pretty special."

"On the train, coming into Lawton, Mama pointed them out to me. They're beautiful!" I smiled. "The last time I was here, I was only three, so I didn't care about mountains."

"Well, they're not the Rockies, that's for sure, but it's enough of a change of scenery that you feel you've been somewhere different. And they're not very far away, so that's the really nice part." He began to tell me all about their history.

Not only did he make it sound exciting, like a good book, but there was something about his voice that made me want to listen to him talk forever. The Wichita Mountains were formed more than 500 million years ago, making them one of the oldest ranges on earth. The Wichita Indians believed that their ancestors came from the rocky summits. All of the Indians of the area, especially the Kiowas and the Comanches, had used them as landmarks as they made their way across the plains. There were also legends of lost mines and hidden treasures. Jesse James and his gang were supposed to have buried some of their bandit loot among the boulders.

"Do you think we could search for it one of these days?" I asked excitedly.

Senator Crawford looked over at me and smiled. "I'd like to do that, Woodrow. Robert asked me the same thing once, but I was too busy at the time, and I kept putting him off." He paused. I saw his Adam's apple bobbing up and down as he swallowed a couple of times. "It would almost make it seem as if I were keeping my promise to him."

We topped a hill, and down in a little valley I saw a town with houses and buildings made of round pink stones. "There's Medicine Park," Senator Crawford said. He told me Medicine Park had been built not only for recreational purposes but also to give Lawton a permanent source of water. "Now people come here from all over, Woodrow, but mostly from Oklahoma and Texas, to enjoy the mountains, the wildlife, the swimming, and the good food and lodging." Again he laughed, and I could tell he was laughing at himself, because he added, "If I sound like a pitchman, Woodrow, it's because I am. Some friends of mine and I are partners in the Apache Inn, where we're going to eat." We crossed over Medicine Creek as we entered the town, and in the distance I could see a large pool, which Senator Crawford told me was Bath Lake. It was surrounded by flower gardens, large trees, footbridges, and grassy areas. "Beautiful, isn't it?" he said as we headed up a hill, past almost-secluded pink stone houses, and out of sight of Bath Lake. "I hope you can come here with me often, Woodrow. I used to bring Robert out here a lot, and . . . well, I . . ." He stopped, took a deep breath, let it out, and then said, "I know I'm sounding, well, kind of *presumptuous*. Do you know that word?"

"Yes, sir. It means you think I might want to do something before you've even asked me."

"That's right, and I'm sorry."

I looked at him. He had tears in his eyes. "I'd love to come out here with you again, sir," I said.

Just then we ran off the road, but Senator Crawford quickly turned the steering wheel and said, "That was close. I almost took out one of those trees, didn't I?"

"Yes, sir, you did."

"Well, we can't have that, Woodrow. Oklahoma doesn't have so many trees that the state can afford to lose one."

I laughed. I thought it was really nice that he hadn't even mentioned what might have happened to his automobile. We went up and down a couple more little hills in the town before Senator Crawford pulled into an empty parking space in front of one of the pink stone buildings, with a long, covered wooden porch in front. A sign over the door read APACHE INN.

"I see most of my friends are already here," Senator Crawford said.

I looked over at him. "I thought it was just going to be the two of us." That sounded childish, I knew, but I suddenly didn't want to share Senator Crawford with anyone else.

We just sat there, neither one of us saying anything, until another big automobile arrived and someone shouted, "George! They're not going to serve you out here, even if you are part owner of the place!"

"That's Buddy Jones, one of the bankers in Lawton, and the young man with him is his son, Jimmy," Senator Crawford said. "Jimmy is your age." He opened his door and got out. "Come on. I want to introduce you to them."

After I shook hands with Mr. Jones, Jimmy grabbed my shoulder with one hand and said, "You'll have to come over to my house soon so I can introduce you to some of the people who'll be in our class at school."

"I'd like that very much," I said.

"Well, it's very important to know who you should be friends with and who you shouldn't."

Before I could ask Jimmy what he meant, the four of us headed into the inn, and Jimmy started talking about what great hamburgers they made there. Since I was getting really hungry, I forgot about everything else and turned my attention to Jimmy's description of how the Apache Inn's hamburgers were put together. "It's supposed to be a secret," he whispered to me as we followed his father and Senator Crawford through the dining room and into a back room, "but I wanted to know what it was, so of course the cook told me."

Several people in the dining room looked up from eating to watch us pass. I could tell they thought we were important, and I liked that. The room we went into wasn't as bright as the dining room, because there were no windows looking out onto the creek. As we entered, everyone stood up and nodded in greeting. No one sat down until the four of us had found our places at the front of the room. It all seemed kind of formal, but for some reason that didn't make me feel uncomfortable, as I had felt at some banquets Mama and I attended with Daddy in Washington.

After we sat down, Senator Crawford looked over, smiled, and said, "I'm glad you're here with me."

"I'm glad too, sir. Jimmy was telling me about the great hamburgers. I think that's what I'm going to order."

Senator Crawford patted my arm. "Well, I don't think you'll be disappointed."

I wasn't. Jimmy said the secret was that they fried the meat in buffalo lard. Whatever it was, it certainly tasted better than any hamburger I had ever had in Washington. When I told Senator Crawford that, he said, "You can only get really good hamburgers in this part of the country, Woodrow. Anywhere else, they're all just imitations."

I wasn't quite sure what would happen when everyone had finished eating. Would Jimmy and I just sit there while Senator Crawford and the other men talked about whatever it was they had to talk about? But Jimmy wiped his mouth and asked, "Are you ready to go swimming?"

That sounded like more fun than listening to the men talk.

"I sure am!" I said, hoping Senator Crawford wouldn't think I was being rude.

"You boys should probably walk around for a while to let your food digest," Mr. Jones said. "There are still several hours of daylight left, so you'll have plenty of time to get in a good swim."

"All right, Father," Jimmy said. He looked over at me. "Come on!"

I started to stand up to follow him, but instead I leaned over to Senator Crawford and whispered, "I didn't bring any money with me. I'm sorry."

"Don't worry about it, Woodrow," he said. He patted me on the shoulder. "It's all been taken care of."

"Well, I'll pay you back. I have some money that I . . ."

"Woodrow, you're my guest. I don't expect you to pay for anything."

"Thank you, sir."

"Woodrow?" Jimmy called.

I looked up and saw that he was already at the door to the private dining room. "Coming," I said.

For the next hour, which didn't feel like an hour at all, Jimmy and I walked from one end of Medicine Park to the other. He pointed out several houses that he said were week-end homes for some of the really powerful men in Oklahoma and Texas. "Nobody bothers them here," he said. When we passed Baird's Health Sanitarium, he added, "My grandparents spend a lot of time taking hot baths at this place. The water is supposed to help their aches and pains."

"Does it?"

"They tell everyone that it does. And they always seem to walk better afterward."

But Jimmy didn't like everyone who came to Medicine Park. He said that he wished people with no morals would stay away. "What do you mean?" I asked him.

He stopped and looked at me. "They're not church people, Woodrow. Don't you go to church?"

"We went sometimes in Washington. But a lot of the time Daddy didn't want to get up on Sunday mornings early enough to go."

"We always go to church," Jimmy said.

"We probably will too," I assured him, although I wasn't at all sure that was true. But it seemed terribly important to Jimmy. "Mama just hasn't mentioned anything about it yet," I added.

As we headed down another street, I saw Bath Lake and the water slide at the bottom of the hill. "I think our food has digested by now," Jimmy said. "Let's go get our swimming trunks. It'll feel good to be in the water."

Even though it was getting late, it was still hot, and there were a lot of people in the pool. Jimmy told me that we were lucky, because the only people there were the right kind of people. I decided he knew what he was talking about, because they were all really nice to us. Jimmy introduced me to some other boys and a couple of girls and to several men and women as well. Everyone seemed pleased to meet me, especially when Jimmy told them that I had come to Medicine Park with Senator Crawford. At times it seemed as though everyone in the pool was acting as if Jimmy and I owned it. When we were climbing up the ladder of the slide, they'd move to one side so we could pass them. Although he wasn't rude about it, Jimmy seemed to expect them to do it, because he climbed past them without saying thank you. I followed him, but I always said thank you. Finally Jimmy looked at the sun, which was getting close to the western horizon, and said, "We'd better go. They're probably finished with their meeting by now." I thought about asking him what kind of meeting, but I realized I really didn't care. It had been such a long time since I'd had so much fun, and I didn't want to think about anything else.

Jimmy and I changed back into our clothes and headed up

the hill to the Apache Inn. Just as we got there, Senator Crawford and Mr. Jones stepped out onto the porch. "We're going on vacation tomorrow, but I'll call you when we get back," Jimmy said. "We'll make plans."

"All right," I told him.

Senator Crawford and Mr. Jones shook hands, then Mr. Jones and Jimmy got into their automobile and drove away. I waved at Jimmy, but I guess he didn't see me.

"Well, do you feel refreshed, Woodrow?" Senator Crawford asked.

"I sure do. That was nice."

"How did you and Jimmy get along?"

"Oh, really well, sir. He's going to call me when they get back from their vacation, so he can introduce me to some of the people who'll be in our class at school."

"I'm happy to hear that, Woodrow. It's important that you get to know the right people."

There it was again: "the right sort of people." Senator Crawford put his arm around me as we walked toward his automobile. "This world is full of people who'll pull you down if you let them. You need to be with your own kind, son. If you associate with Godless people, Woodrow, you'll be tainted, and you don't want that, do you?"

"Well, sir, Mama always tells me to look for the good in everybody, so I'll probably just keep doing that."

Senator Crawford smiled but didn't say anything more. We got into his car and headed out of Medicine Park. I was suddenly sleepy, and what I really wanted to do then was lean back and take a nap, but I blinked a couple of times and forced myself to stay awake. "Good-bye, Medicine Park," I said.

"You don't have to say 'good-bye,' Woodrow, just 'see you later,' because we'll be out here again before you know it." Senator Crawford looked over at me. "Would you like that?"

"Oh yes, sir! I had a wonderful time."

chapter SIX

All the windows of Senator Crawford's automobile were down, and I was enjoying just lying against the warm seat with my eyes closed as we drove back to Lawton. I must have fallen asleep, because the next thing I knew, the sun had set and we were pulling into Senator Crawford's garage. Senator Crawford turned off the engine, but he didn't open his door to get out. "I'm sorry," I said with a yawn. "That was rude of me."

"That's all right, Woodrow. I know all that exercise must have made you sleepy."

"It really did, sir. Well, good night."

"Wait, Woodrow. There's something I want to ask you."

I turned to look at him. "Yes, sir?"

"What do you miss most about your father?"

"I miss having one."

"When someone is suddenly taken away from you, it's hard to understand why, even for people who know in their hearts that God had a reason for doing it."

I nodded. "It was especially hard for Mama."

"I was told that a Negro man was driving the other car. Is that true?"

"Yes, sir."

Senator Crawford shook his head. "That's really ironic, Woodrow. Your father liked Negroes. He thought they should have the same rights as white people in this country. I wonder what he would think about Negroes now."

That seemed like a strange thing to say. "I don't think the accident had anything to do with who was driving, sir," I said. "It wasn't really the Negro man's fault."

Senator Crawford shrugged. "Well, we'd better get out, Woodrow, or people will probably think something has happened to us. The next time you come over, I'll show you some of my other paintings, and if you want to, we can even start painting something together."

"I've always wanted to paint flowers," I said without thinking, "because . . ." I hesitated, fearing I'd see in Senator

Crawford's eyes the same disinterest I had seen in Daddy's when I talked about painting, but it wasn't there.

"I like to paint flowers too, Woodrow. There are some beautiful wildflowers out in the mountains. Maybe one of these days we could paint some of them together."

"Could we?"

"If it's all right with your mother."

"I don't think she'll care, but . . ."

"But *what*, Woodrow?"

"Well, Mama's having a really hard time dealing with Daddy's death, and most of the time I don't know what to say to her. I want to help her, but . . . I don't want to be the way she is."

Senator Crawford nodded. "That's how my wife was after Robert died, Woodrow, and I felt the same way you do now. I wanted to help her, but I also wanted to get on with my own life." He leaned up close and looked me in the eyes. "Remember this, Woodrow," he whispered, "you can always talk to me about anything that's troubling you."

I was about to respond when somebody rapped on the driver's-side door, startling us both, and we turned our heads in unison. In the dim light, I could barely make out Benjamin's face. "Dumb coon!" Senator Crawford muttered, surprising me.

"What does he want?" He opened the door, pinning Benjamin against the side of the garage. "What do you mean, scaring the hell out of me like that, boy?"

Senator Crawford sounded like a totally different person when he shouted at Benjamin, but I told myself that sometimes people say things they don't mean when they're startled.

"I'm sorry, Senator," Benjamin said. "Mr. Woodrow's mother has called twice. She wanted to know if you had come back from Medicine Park."

Senator Crawford turned back to me. "I'll go in with you, Woodrow, so I can apologize for keeping you out so late."

"You don't really have to."

"Well, this will be a good excuse to meet your mother."

We got out of the automobile. When Senator Crawford shut his door, I realized that Benjamin had still been behind it, pinned against the wall.

Mary didn't say anything when she opened the door for Senator Crawford and me. I thought she looked scared. Finally, she murmured, "Good evening, Senator," but she never once looked at him.

"Where's Mama?" I asked as Senator Crawford and I stepped inside the house.

"She's up in her room."

"Senator Crawford wants to—" I started to say, but Senator Crawford put his hand on my arm and said, "Oh, I probably shouldn't disturb her now, Woodrow."

Just then we all turned as we heard Mama coming down the stairs. She was carrying a couple of dresses. When she saw us, she said, "I thought I heard voices. I was getting worried about you, Woodrow."

Senator Crawford started walking toward her. "I'm George Crawford, Mrs. Harper, and this is all my fault. We were having such a good time, I forgot how late it was."

Mama had reached the last step. "Mary, would you wash these things for me tomorrow morning?"

"Yes, Mrs. Harper." Mary walked over, took the dresses from Mama, and headed toward the kitchen.

Mama offered her hand to Senator Crawford. "I'm Peggy Harper. It's a pleasure to meet you, Senator."

"The pleasure is mine, Mrs. Harper." Senator Crawford nodded his head toward me. "I think Woodrow would agree that we had a wonderful time at Medicine Park, but I want to apologize if I caused you any concern."

"I was afraid that something might have happened to you. I worry about automobile accidents since what happened to Woodrow's father in Washington."

"Yes, I heard about your tragedy, ma'am," Senator Crawford said, "and I want to offer you my condolences."

At that moment Joshua appeared at the door to the kitchen. When Senator Crawford saw him, his face turned bright red.

Mama was staring at Senator Crawford. "Thank you for taking Woodrow to Medicine Park," she said, but she didn't sound very friendly. "Good night."

Senator Crawford nodded. "Good night, Mrs. Harper." He put his hand on my shoulder and said, "Good night, Woodrow."

"Good night. The next time I come over to your house, I'll—"

"Woodrow!" Mama said sharply. "Go on up to your room! And, Joshua, you go back into the kitchen!"

Joshua quickly disappeared. Instead of moving, I watched Senator Crawford leave the house.

"Woodrow?" Mama said.

I turned back to her. "You were rude to him! He was nice to me, and you were rude to him!"

"Do what I told you to do! Now! Do you understand me?"

"Yes, ma'am," I said.

When I got to my room, I walked over to the window that looked out onto Senator Crawford's house. He was going up the steps of his front porch. I tried to picture myself inside, the two of us talking about things, maybe painting pictures of flowers, while Benjamin brought us lemonade. I decided to get ready for bed, but then I heard sobbing coming from Mama's room. All my anger left me, and I knew that I had to go to her. She was sitting on the side of her bed, staring up at the pictures of Daddy on the walls. "Mama?" I said.

Mama turned and looked at me. Her eyes were full of tears and seemed unfocused, and for a moment I wasn't even sure she recognized who I was. But then her eyes took on a glow that I remembered from before Daddy died and she said, "I am so sorry I yelled at you, Woodrow." She stood up and opened her arms to embrace me. "It's just the two of us now, and we have to take care of each other. Your father would have wanted it that way. You have to promise me that you'll never forget him. We have to keep his memory alive." Now Mama was holding me so tight that I could hardly breathe. "We have to be true to him, Woodrow," she continued. "There were things about him that you don't know, good things, but things that caused him some grief when he was your age. You're going to have to make some difficult choices in life, and I want you to make sure you lead your life the way your father would have wanted you to."

"I'll try, Mama."

When I got back to my room, I turned out the light, but instead of getting into bed, I walked back into the hallway so I could look out the window once again at Senator Crawford's house. There was a light on in one of the rooms and through the drawn shades I could see the shadow of a man as he paced back and forth.

chapter SEVEN

When I woke up the next morning, I was still thinking about Senator Crawford. For the first time in my life, I'd met a grown man who seemed to take me and what I wanted to do seriously, and I found myself wondering what it would have been like if my father had felt that way. The thoughts made me feel guilty, and I tried to push them away.

The legislature was in session, and Senator Crawford was staying in his house in Oklahoma City, so I didn't see him for some time after our dinner at Medicine Park. Mama and I drifted back into our routine. We went shopping—mostly, I decided, just to have something to fill our days. Once in a while

I'd go with Mama to her classroom at Lawton High School, where she seemed to only move books and papers back to the places they were the last time we were there. She kept saying that she was sure she'd feel better once school started and it wasn't so hot, but I don't think she really believed that. I wasn't sure I did either.

We got our new automobile, and we drove it all around Lawton and out into the countryside. Once we even went to Fort Sill, but it really seemed to upset Mama, so we never did that again. That day, though, on the trip back to our house, I was sure that I saw Senator Crawford sitting in the backseat of a long black automobile as it sped past us. But it went by so fast, I couldn't be sure, and when I didn't see him at his house that night, I wondered if my eyes had just been playing tricks on me.

The next morning I awakened to see Mama standing at the door of my bedroom.

"Woodrow?"

I sat up. "Yes, ma'am?"

"It's time to get up. Mary has breakfast waiting for you."

I put my feet down on the hardwood floor and stood up. "Mama, I sure do miss Senator Crawford."

"Woodrow, you had just one dinner with the man. You should be meeting people your own age."

"That's just it, Mama, he can help me do that. I met Jimmy Jones when the senator took me to Medicine Park. He's my age. We even went swimming together in Bath Lake." I filled her in on everything that Jimmy and I had done. "His father is an important banker here in Lawton, and Jimmy and I got along really well. He wants to introduce me to some of the people who are going to be in my class at school this year." I could tell that Mama was thinking about what I had just said. "It's important that I get to know the right people here in Lawton," I continued, "and with Senator Crawford, that's what—"

"What do you mean, the *right* people, Woodrow?" Mama interrupted me.

"Well, the *nice* people, churchgoing people, the people who think the same way that we think," I told her, trying to remember everything that Jimmy had said. "I guess there are some people in Lawton who aren't very nice, that you don't want to know, because they'll drag you down to their level."

"Oh, Woodrow! What kind of *nice*, *churchgoing* people would be so condemning? I'm not sure this Jimmy Jones is the kind of friend your father would want you to be making."

"But he was very nice to me, Mama, and I could tell other kids looked up to him. He'll help me make friends when—"

"We need to talk about this, Woodrow," Mama said, interrupting me again. "But Mary is waiting for you. Go on."

When I got downstairs, Mary set my breakfast on the table. Ham, scrambled eggs, biscuits, gravy, and apple butter. I started eating, and she went back to washing dishes. After a few minutes, I said, "I haven't seen Joshua in a while. What's he doing?"

"He's helping out with some livestock on Mr. Fuller's farm. I told him if he finishes early to come by here." Mary turned and looked at me. "Mr. Woodrow, I know this is asking a lot, but I surely would be happy if you'd spend some time talking to Joshua, setting him straight about things. I don't want him falling in with the wrong people and getting into any more trouble than he already has. Would you think about doing that for me?"

My mouth was full, so I just nodded, but I suddenly wondered if Mary and Jimmy meant the same thing by *wrong* people and *right* people.

The ringing telephone interrupted my thoughts. Mary dried her hands on a tea towel and went to answer it. I heard her say, "Just a minute, please, sir." When she came back into the kitchen, she said, "It's for you, Mr. Woodrow. It's that young Mr. Jones."

I jumped up from the table, ran down the hall, and grabbed the receiver. "Welcome home!" I said.

"Was that your nigra?" Jimmy said.

"Yes."

"Well, your mama needs to talk to her. No nigra should ever talk to a white person like that. She was surly."

"I'm sure she didn't mean to be, Jimmy."

"Oh, don't let nigras fool you, Woodrow. They don't like white people, and you always have to watch out for them and make sure they don't overstep their bounds. You need to remember that."

What Jimmy was saying made me think about how Joshua had annoyed me with his attitude the day I met him. "You're right," I told him.

"I know I'm right, Woodrow. Anyway, I didn't call you to talk about your nigra. I called you to let you know that we were back from our vacation, and if you're not busy, I can be over in a few minutes."

"That's great! I'll be waiting for you." I hung up the receiver and went back into the kitchen. "Could I have some more of those biscuits with apple butter, Mary?"

Mary nodded. She took the pan of biscuits out of the oven, buttered a couple, and then put them on a plate in front of me. "Is that young Mr. Jones coming over here?" she asked.

"Yes. I met him when Senator Crawford took me to

Medicine Park. He's going to help me meet the right people in Lawton."

Mary got a funny look on her face. "Is that so? Well, I hope they're all as 'right' as you want them to be, Mr. Woodrow." She looked up at the clock on the wall. "If you're finished, I need to wash those dishes, so I can run my errands."

I stood up. "I'm finished. Thanks, Mary."

"You're welcome, Mr. Woodrow," Mary said. Then she stopped me at the door with "Mr. Woodrow, your daddy may not have been perfect, but he was a nice man, and he treated us colored folks like human beings."

First Mama, now Mary. Why didn't they understand my father wasn't around anymore? I needed someone else to help me find a place for myself in Lawton.

I was in my room when I heard the knocker. Mary had already left, and Mama had gone back to bed, so I went downstairs and opened the front door. Jimmy was standing there looking as though he was going to church. "Where's your nigra?" he said.

"What?"

"Why did you open the front door yourself? Why didn't you let your nigra do it?"

"She's gone. She had some errands to run."

Jimmy came in. "Nigras always have some excuse to get out of work, don't they?" He looked around. "This is a nice old house. My father said he was glad that some Harpers were living in it again. He's afraid that some of these big old homes will be turned into boardinghouses, and that won't be good for us, he said."

"Mama and I think it's a nice house too. I'll show you my room. It's upstairs."

"Okay."

When we got there, the first thing Jimmy did was point to the framed picture of Daddy on top of my dresser. "Is that your father?" he asked.

"Yes," I told him.

"My father said your father liked nigras. Did you know that?"

I nodded.

"I don't have a picture of my father on my dresser. I have one of Jesus Christ." He looked at me. "I could get you one too."

That sounded kind of strange to me, so I said, "I had this on my dresser back in Washington, so I wanted to have it here too. I don't think there's really room for another picture."

"If you're a Christian, you need to let people know

about it right away, Woodrow. Have you ever heard of the Crusades?"

"Yes. I read a book about them once."

"Reverend Clark says we're fighting a crusade in this country right now. That's the kind of soldier I want to be, a soldier of Jesus Christ, and I think . . ." Jimmy suddenly looked as though somebody had hit him in the face. He was staring wide-eyed at the door. I turned and saw Joshua standing there. "What's he doing here?" Jimmy demanded.

"That's Joshua. His mother asked me—"

"I know who he is. It's your nigra's boy. What's he doing here?" He turned to me. "You shouldn't let niggers come up to your room, Woodrow."

After that, everything happened so fast. Joshua flew across the room at Jimmy and they both fell to the wooden floor with a heavy thud. Jimmy groaned in pain, and Joshua started pummeling him in the face. Jimmy tried his best to fend off the blows, but Joshua was stronger. At first I just stood there, but then I grabbed Joshua by his collar and tried to pull him off. I only managed to tear his shirt.

"Stop it!" Mama was at my door, and there was more life in her eyes than I'd seen in a week. "Stop it!" she screamed again, her mouth twisted angrily. This time Joshua stopped hitting Jimmy, but he didn't move from on top of him. "Get up, Joshua!" Mama told him. "Now!" Joshua did as he was told, and I could see in his eyes that he knew he had made a serious mistake. He kept his head down and refused to look at Mama. "What is going on in here, Woodrow?" she demanded.

I opened my mouth to explain, but before I could, Joshua shouted, "He called me a nigger!"

"That's what you are!" Jimmy said through bloody lips.

Joshua made a move to resume the fight, but Mama said, "Stop it, Joshua! Go to the kitchen and stay there until I come down." As Joshua hurried out of the room, Mama turned to me and said, "Woodrow, there's a bottle of iodine in the bathroom. Go get it and bring me one of the face cloths."

I did as I was told, but when I got back to the room, Jimmy was gone and Mama was sitting on the side of my bed. "Where's Jimmy?"

"He left."

"Did he say he'd come back later?" I asked, and thought right away how stupid that sounded.

Mama shook her head.

I looked around my room and all I saw was Daddy staring at me with sad and disapproving eyes. I had to get out of there so I could breathe. Somehow, my thoughts turned to Senator

Crawford. I was sure I had seen him getting out of that long black car the night before, so I knew he was home. I left my room without saying anything to Mama, because I didn't know what to say. When I got outside, I took the front porch steps two at a time and ran across our yard to Senator Crawford's house. "I have to talk to Senator Crawford," I told Benjamin when he answered my knock.

Behind Benjamin, in the darkness of the room, Senator Crawford said, "Please come in, Woodrow."

Benjamin held open the door for me. When my eyes adjusted to the light, I saw Jimmy sitting in one of the chairs. He was holding a cloth up against his lips.

"You go on home now, Jimmy," Senator Crawford said. "Everything will be taken care of."

Jimmy stood up and walked past me. "I'm sorry," I said to him. He didn't look at me, but he nodded, and he didn't seem angry.

"It's all right, Woodrow," Senator Crawford said. "Jimmy and I had a long talk. He knows that what happened wasn't your fault." Benjamin let Jimmy out the front door and closed it behind him. "Benjamin, bring us some lemonade." Senator Crawford put his arm around my shoulders and led me into his study. "Let's sit down and take a load off our feet."

"It's so peaceful in here. I feel really happy when I'm in this house . . ." I stopped and swallowed hard as Benjamin came into the study with a pitcher of lemonade and two glasses. "*And with you,*" I added in a whisper when Benjamin was gone.

"I'm glad you feel that way, Woodrow."

I knew then that I didn't need to be embarrassed by how I felt toward Senator Crawford. It was as if a very heavy load had been lifted from my shoulders. "I didn't want Joshua to come over, but Mary asked me this morning if I would talk to him," I told him, "and I didn't know what to say, Senator Crawford, I really didn't."

"I know, I know," Senator Crawford said. He took another sip of lemonade. "Doesn't Benjamin make good lemonade? It's so refreshing. I've tried to imitate it, but I just can never quite get it right, and old Benjamin, well, he's rather protective of his recipe." For several minutes, we didn't say anything to each other; we just drank our lemonade and listened to the ticking of the grandfather clock in the corner of the room. Finally Senator Crawford set his glass on the table and turned to me. "Why do you think Joshua and Jimmy had their fight?" he asked.

I shrugged. "Well, Jimmy was kind of mean to Joshua. He called him a bad name."

Senator Crawford smiled and shook his head. "No, no,

that's not it at all. You may have thought he was being mean, but Jimmy understands what has to be done, and it's very important that you understand that too, Woodrow."

"But I *don't* understand, sir."

Senator Crawford put his hand on my shoulder. "It'll just take some time, but I promise you that it won't be long until you realize the truth." He stood up. "I think we need to start our painting lessons now."

chapter EIGHT

Senator Crawford led me to his solarium, a large glassed-in room where the temperature was controlled so he could grow tropical flowers year-round. It was very hot and humid. Everywhere I looked, there were flowers of all colors, shapes, and sizes, but I didn't recognize any of them. "They're so beautiful," I said. "What are they?"

"Orchids, and some of these you'll only find in the jungles of South America. It's my private world, Woodrow. Because of all the foliage in my backyard, very few people are even aware this room is here, and even fewer people have been inside."

"Do you sell them?"

Senator Crawford shook his head. "No, Woodrow, I paint

them. Once in a while I give some away to friends, but more often than not, I leave them here, because I don't like to see them die any sooner than they naturally would." He looked at me. "Flowers are such a perfect example of God's marvelous handiwork. It's a pity that some of his human creations seem so flawed by comparison."

For the next few minutes, we simply wandered around. When we finally reached the back of the solarium, I saw two easels and two tall stools. "This is where you and I will paint our masterpieces, Woodrow, and when your painting is finished, it'll hang in my house, and, if you want, my painting can hang in your room."

"What if my painting doesn't turn out very well? You may not want to have it in your house."

"Oh, don't worry, I'll be with you every step of the way to make sure that what you're doing turns out the way you want it to. I'm going to teach you everything you need to know, and I'm sure it will be perfect." He talked about pigments, additives, color, painting techniques, light, brushes, paper, and solvents until my head was swimming. "But don't think you have to remember all of this at once. We'll take everything just a little bit at a time."

We spent the next two hours doing the underpainting.

When Benjamin interrupted us with "I have lunch ready, Senator," I couldn't believe the time had passed so quickly.

As we left the solarium and entered Senator Crawford's house, I was suddenly transported back to of what had happened that morning. "Maybe I should go on home. Mary may be back from her errands, and she's probably upset with me because I didn't keep Joshua out of trouble like I told her I would."

"I wouldn't worry about Mary. She's had enough trouble from that son of hers that she should expect it by now. You should think about yourself, about what the future holds for you, and not concern yourself with problems that aren't of your making."

"But I . . ." Suddenly that seemed easier than trying to deal with what had happened, so I said, "All right."

Halfway through lunch, though, Senator Crawford stopped eating and said, "Woodrow, I can see that your mind is still on what happened this morning, because you've just been picking at your food. Maybe you should go on home after all."

I looked up at him. "You're not angry with me, are you?"

"No, Woodrow, I'm not angry." Senator Crawford wiped his mouth with his napkin. "It's just going to take some time for you to realize that there are certain things you don't need to worry about. Now, run along, but please come back later so I can be sure that you're all right."

Benjamin was standing at the front door to let me out.

"I'll be back," I told him.

"Yes, sir, Mr. Woodrow."

I jumped off the front porch and ran across the lawn to our back door so I could go in through the kitchen. Mama and Mary were sitting at the table. They looked up with a start when I came in. I could tell that Mary had been crying. "Woodrow, Joshua seems to have disappeared," Mama said. "Did he tell you where he was going?"

I shook my head. "But you don't need to worry about what happened, Mary. Jimmy was at Senator Crawford's house when I went over there, and Senator Crawford said everything was going to be all right."

Mary turned and looked up at me. "Oh, Mr. Woodrow, you just don't understand. It won't be all right either." She stood up. "I have to go see if maybe my boy is at home, Mrs. Harper. I have to go make sure that nothing bad has happened to him."

We didn't see Mary for three days, and Mama seemed more depressed than ever. I wanted to go back over to Senator Crawford's house to finish my painting, but I knew that would make her feel worse. Except for meals, we mostly stayed in our bedrooms. Finally, on the fourth day, Mary was in the kitchen when I went down to breakfast. She was preparing a tray to take up to Mama, she told me.

"Is she sick?" I asked, worried.

"No, Mr. Woodrow, I just think she's really tired, and she's not eating enough. But Miss Winifred is coming to take her to a doctor today just to make sure everything's all right."

I stood up from the table. "I'll carry the tray up to her."

"Mr. Woodrow, you just sit down here and eat your breakfast." Mary set my plate firmly on the table, and I knew she meant what she said. "There's really nothing you can do for your mama except keep her from worrying about you."

"Why would she be worrying about me?"

Mary didn't answer my question. Instead she said, "I'll go on and take this tray up now, Mr. Woodrow."

I had almost finished eating when there was a knock on the front door. Mary let Winifred into the house and together they went upstairs. After a few minutes, I heard the three of them coming downstairs. Mama's face looked so pale that I thought Mary hadn't told me the truth. "Mama? What's wrong?"

"Nothing's wrong, Woodrow," Winifred said. She had

Mama by one of her arms and was helping her down the last few steps. "Your mama is going to be fine."

I just stood and stared at them as they left the house.

"I know your mama looked kind of peaked, Mr. Woodrow," Mary said, "but Miss Winifred will take care of her."

She was halfway to the kitchen when I said, "Did you find Joshua?"

Mary stopped and turned around slowly. "He hopped a freight train to Chicago so he could stay with his uncle. He left a note telling me he'd be all right and for me not to worry about him." She gave me a big smile. "I'm sorry I got so upset, Mr. Woodrow. No matter what you may hear from some of the people here in Lawton, Joshua is a fine boy, he is. You mark my word." With that she disappeared into the kitchen.

It seemed kind of strange that Mary wasn't upset about Joshua riding a freight train all the way to Chicago. I knew Mama would have been if I had done something like that. But I figured Mary was probably just relieved that Joshua was out of Lawton.

I spent the rest of the day in my room wondering what it would be like to ride a freight train to another town like Joshua. I found a map of the United States that had railroad lines marked on it and imagined myself traveling to different cities all over the country. I had just arrived in Seattle, Washington, and was looking for a place to stay when I noticed Mary standing at my door.

"Miss Winifred just called and said that the doctor gave your mama an iron shot, because she's anemic, but she's going to be all right. They'll be home in a few minutes."

"Oh, that's wonderful news, Mary." I stood up. "Well, I think I'll go over and visit Senator Crawford."

"Mr. Woodrow, I wish you wouldn't. I don't think your mama would want you to . . ."

But I was down the stairs and out the front door before Mary could finish. My heart was pounding when I reached Senator Crawford's front porch, wondering how he'd act toward me after so much time, but just as I raised my fist to knock, the door opened and Senator Crawford was standing there. "Woodrow!" he said. "What a nice surprise!"

"You're not angry with me?"

"Of course not! I could never be angry with you, Woodrow. You're just like my . . ." He hesitated and didn't finish his sentence, but he put his arms around me and hugged me. We stayed that way for several moments more, and the warmth of his body and the smell of the soap he used helped calm me down. After I told him about Mama, he said, "I have an idea. Let's take her some of my flowers. Would you like that?"

I looked up at him. "You'd give Mama some of your flowers, even after she was so rude to you?"

"Of course, Woodrow. I understand what your mother's going through, son. Remember that I went through the same thing myself, twice, with the death of Robert and then of his mother."

"Thank you, Senator Crawford. I really do love her, but I don't understand what's happening to her."

"She probably doesn't understand it either, Robert."

I looked at him. "You just called me Robert."

"Did I? I didn't realize that I had. I'm sorry."

"I don't mind. I really don't."

Senator Crawford smiled. "Let's go cut the flowers, all right?"

"All right. I know what colors Mama likes."

As we headed toward the solarium, Senator Crawford said, "Is Joshua, by any chance, over at your house?"

"No. Mary said he went to Chicago to live with his uncle. I guess he took that freight train up there after all."

Senator Crawford stopped. "You're sure that's what she said?"

I nodded. "Yes, sir." The look on his face was the same as when he first saw Joshua at our house, and I suddenly wondered what he *really* wanted to know. "Why?"

Now he smiled. "I was just curious, that's all."

Benjamin put the flowers in a crystal vase, and the senator and I took them next door to my house. He told me that he'd wait downstairs while I went up to Mama's room.

Winifred was sitting in a big chair pulled up alongside Mama's bed. Mama had her eyes closed.

"How absolutely lovely," Winifred said in a quiet voice when she saw the flowers. "Where did you get these orchids?"

"It's a secret."

One of Winifred's eyebrows went up. "Well, we'll just keep it a secret, then," she said. She took the flowers from me and set them on a table.

Just then Mama opened her eyes. For a moment she seemed startled, but Winifred took her hand, patted it, and said, "Look who's here, Peggy."

Mama moved her head slightly, saw me, and smiled. I went over to the side of the bed. "Are you feeling better?" I asked.

"Yes, sweetheart, I really am."

I leaned down and kissed her cheek. It felt kind of damp and unpleasant, and I suddenly didn't want to stay in the room any longer than I had to. I backed away from Mama's bed, but she didn't seem to notice, as Winifred had taken over the conversation. After a couple of minutes, I said, "Bye, Mama! Get some rest!" I felt guilty for thinking it, but I was hoping she wouldn't call me over to her bed to kiss her good-bye, because I didn't want to feel that damp skin on my lips again. "I'll see you later."

"All right," Mama said.

Winifred squeezed Mama's hand. "Now, don't you worry about anything, Peggy. Everything is going to be just fine."

I left Mama's room and ran downstairs to Senator Crawford. "I want to go back to your house," I told him.

chapter NINE

At our front door, Senator Crawford said, "I've got an errand to do tonight, and I'll be in Oklahoma City for a few days, so it might be better if you stayed here." He patted my shoulder. "I'll call you soon."

"All right," I said, trying not to show my disappointment.

Just as I turned around, Mary was coming down the stairs. "I'll be in the kitchen if you need anything, Mr. Woodrow."

"Thank you, Mary."

I got upstairs just in time to see Senator Crawford backing the Buick Touring out of the garage. I wondered where he was going and why he didn't want to tell me.

* * *

When I passed Mama's room the next morning, she was sitting up in bed eating breakfast. She called me to her, and I went in. I was amazed at how much food Mary had put on her tray, but Mama seemed to be eating it all. She wanted to discuss our plans for the next few days. She had already met one of my teachers, Mrs. Wrenn, who happened to be the wife of the principal at Lawton High School, and she was sure that I was going to enjoy being in the seventh grade. She told me to go downstairs and eat while she got dressed, and then we'd go over to her classroom and finish getting it ready. After that, she said, we'd go shopping for my school clothes. I had hoped Jimmy would have called me by now—so I could find out what everyone usually wore and maybe meet the people he said he'd introduce me to—but he hadn't. I was afraid he was angry with me after all about what Joshua had done to him, but I pushed those worries aside and tried to focus on the fact that Mama really did seem to be getting better.

A few nights later I was lying in bed, staring up at the moonlit ceiling and thinking about school starting, when I heard a noise outside my room. Was Mama having trouble sleeping? I got up and crept out into the hallway. There was enough light from the window at the end for me to see the outline of someone standing at the top of the stairs. "Mama?" I asked.

For a moment, the figure didn't move, but when the person started walking toward me, I could tell it wasn't Mama.

"Who's—," I started to say, but a voice whispered angrily, "Be quiet!"

I recognized Joshua's voice, and just as I started to breathe normally again, I remembered that he was supposed to be in Chicago with his uncle. "When did you get back?" I asked when he reached me.

"I never went anywhere. My mama just told you that."

"Why?"

"Because that's what she wanted certain other people to believe."

"What *certain* other people?"

"Well, to start with, Jimmy Jones and his old man," Joshua said.

"Were you afraid that Mr. Jones might be angry at you because you beat up Jimmy?" When Joshua didn't answer me, I said, "Where have you been all this time?"

"Hiding in a friend's house."

His answer really took me aback. "Then, what are you doing at our house now?"

"His family was too scared for me to be at theirs, so they said I had to leave. My mama told me to sleep in your attic tonight until we can decide what to do. But I got hungry, so I was going to the kitchen to get something to eat." For a couple of minutes, Joshua just stood there in the dark, staring at me. "Are you going to tell anyone where I am?"

"No." *But I should,* I thought, suddenly angry at how Mary and Joshua had been lying to Mama and me.

"You'd better not, because you'd get my mama in trouble if you did, and your mama would fire her, and then we wouldn't have any money to live on. She's the only one who . . ." He stopped.

"I know. Winifred told us that your daddy drinks and can't keep a job." It was a mean thing to say, but Joshua's attitude was really starting to get to me.

"You probably think all *nigger* men are just like my daddy, don't you?"

"I didn't say that."

"You didn't have to, but you're thinking it."

"Don't tell me what I'm thinking. You don't know everything!"

Joshua raised his fists. "I know a lot more than you do, white boy!"

For just a moment, I wanted to put Joshua in his place. But I knew I couldn't beat Joshua in a fight any more than Jimmy could—Joshua was used to fighting and I wasn't. "Is that all you people ever do?" I asked, angry with myself for letting a Negro boy frighten me. "Don't you know how to settle problems without fighting?"

Joshua didn't answer my question right away, but when he finally did, what he said surprised me. "It's all we have."

"What do you mean, 'it's all you have'? I've never been in a fight in my life."

"You didn't have to tell me that."

Again I wanted to remind Joshua that a Negro shouldn't talk to me like that, the way Jimmy would have, but something kept me from doing it. I didn't really think it was because I was afraid of him. "Why don't you answer my question? What makes you think it's all you have?"

"Because no white man is going to listen to what a Negro has to say. He still thinks we just got off one of those slave ships from Africa, and he's afraid that if he looks away for a minute, we're going to throw a spear at him. So that's the only thing we've got, Woodrow, that fear."

"Well, I'm listening now," I said.

"What?" Joshua said.

"I said I'm listening. What is it that you want to tell me?"

I heard a slight intake of breath, then Joshua said, "Do you remember those Klansmen we saw from the attic, the ones who were walking up and down in front of that house?"

"I remember."

"That's the Wilsons' house, and they have a colored woman who cooks for them named Darcy Miller. Her son Theodore, the one I told you about, well, he talked to a white girl downtown one Saturday night. The Klan wanted to punish him, but he ran away before they could. So those Klansmen told Mr. Wilson not to let Darcy work for him until she told them where Theodore was."

"They wanted to punish Theodore just for *talking* to the girl?" I asked. It didn't make sense.

"Well, he smiled at her too, but only after she smiled at him. I know Theodore, and he wouldn't do anything to get himself in trouble. But somebody saw it happen, and they told the Klan. Now the Klan's going to punish Theodore tonight, and then Darcy can go back to work tomorrow for the Wilsons."

"Did Darcy really tell the Klan where Theodore was?"

Joshua nodded.

"Maybe Darcy thought Theodore deserved to be punished for what he did."

"No, she didn't! But she didn't have any other choice. Brother Miller, that's Darcy's husband, lost his job at the dairy, and they have a lot of kids, so she needed to keep her job."

"How do you know all this?"

"Because us colored folks talk to each other about these things, that's why."

"I can't believe the Klan would do that just because Theodore smiled at a white girl."

Even in the dim moonlight, I could see the angry flash in Joshua's eyes. "You need to pay more attention to what's happening around here," he snapped. "We could sneak out and go watch them, and maybe then you'll believe it."

"Maybe they're just going to *talk* to Theodore," I said.

Joshua shook his head in disgust. "Most white people, like you, don't want to accept the truth about the Klan. Talking is not the way they punish colored people."

He turned to leave. When I put my hand on his shoulder to stop him, he jerked it away, but then, without saying anything, he turned back to face me. "I'll go with you," I said.

I got dressed and followed Joshua downstairs. As we went out the front door, the grandfather clock chimed eleven. We had gone only a few blocks when Joshua said, "We'll cut through this backyard here. Squaw Creek is right behind it, and it flows through where the Klan has all of its meetings."

"All right," I said. As we started toward a wooden gate, though, I heard a dog bark, and I stopped.

"Old Bruno is in the yard next door, not in Mrs. Fulton's, so he won't bother us," Joshua said. "But we need to hurry, because Mrs. Fulton always comes out with her shotgun to see if there's a prowler if Bruno barks too long." Joshua opened the back gate and waited until I was through before shutting it. "From here on, we have to be very careful," he whispered, "because it's not only the Klan we have to watch out for; it's snakes and chiggers and ticks too."

"Don't worry about me," I told him.

"It's not you I'm worried about—it's me. I'm just telling you so you'll know not to make a lot of noise, no matter what happens."

With that, Joshua headed through the waist-high grass that bordered Squaw Creek behind Mrs. Fulton's back fence. When we reached the bank, the grass wasn't as tall, and the ground was pretty hard because it hadn't rained in a while. Squaw Creek wasn't much of a creek, either. I could see the moonlight reflecting off only puddles of water. It kind of stank, too. Joshua kept up a steady pace. We went under several wooden bridges and once in a while we had to stop and duck down in the grass as an automobile crossed over one of them. Finally Joshua said, "From here, Squaw Creek heads south. Don't talk, and be ready to run if I tell you to."

When I saw the burning cross through the trees, it took my breath away. The first thing that came to mind was how beautiful it looked. "What do we do now?" I whispered.

"We keep following the creek bank, because it'll lead us right to where they always meet." Joshua turned to face me. "But if you're scared, we can go back now, because—"

"Why would I be scared?" I said, interrupting him.

"I was just wanting to make sure, that's all, because I don't want you getting us into trouble."

I was glad to see that, just beyond the creek bank, in the direction of the cross, a border of large trees, smaller bushes, and tall grass would keep us hidden. It wasn't long before we could not only see the cross better but also hear the hum of voices. It took a lot of people to make that much noise, I knew, and then I saw something that awed me more than the burning cross had. There were hundreds of Klansmen in their white robes and hoods milling around in an open pasture. When Joshua didn't move, I said, "I want to get closer." Joshua shook his head, but I continued. "I can't tell much about what's going on from here. We can at least go as far as the tree line."

When Joshua still hadn't moved after a few minutes, I started up the creek bank, but Joshua grabbed my arm and pulled me back. "It's never been this big before," he whispered.

"How many times have you been out here?" I asked him.

"Three, maybe four, times."

"That's not many. Maybe they've had a lot of big meetings like this and you just weren't here." I jerked my arm away from Joshua and started back up the creek bank. This time he followed. At the edge of the trees, the bushes and grass continued right up to what I now could tell was a barbed-wire fence.

"We can get down on our knees and crawl from here," Joshua said.

In the center of the pasture, the huge wooden cross continued to burn, sending an eerie light flickering out around it. There were four smaller crosses at the corners of the pasture, illuminating the space around them. I held my breath when some Klansmen passed right in front of us and stopped to smoke cigarettes.

"There are only three things in this world that are important to me," one of the men said. "Kluxing, preserving the purity of white women, and doing anything else Jesus wants us to do."

"Well, those things are important to me too, brother, but I'd add one more thing," the other Klansman said. He snickered. "A good smoke, because I can't do without my tobacco."

"Well, I can take it or leave it," the first Klansman said, "because I don't think Jesus smoked." He flicked his cigarette butt into the grass and it landed on Joshua's hand. He jerked his hand away and the grass rustled, making the Klansman whirl around. "What was that?" he said.

"Just some animal," the other one said. "Squaw Creek runs behind my house too, and there are all kinds of them back there." He tossed his unfinished cigarette out into the grass too, and it landed between me and Joshua. "Come on, it's about to start, and I don't want to miss any of this."

The Klansmen were now all standing in military formation in each of the four corners of the pasture. Suddenly, the hum of voices stopped, and it was so quiet I was sure if I moved even an inch they would hear me.

A Klansman dressed in a bright purple robe and hood walked out in front of the large burning cross with two other Klansmen beside him. One was dressed in a red robe and hood and the other in a blue robe and hood. They were obviously some sort of leaders.

The Klansman in purple held out one hand toward the audience and said something I couldn't quite hear, but the rest of the Klansmen around the pasture responded. Then, from each of the four groups, several Klansmen stepped forward and stood in front of the leaders.

The Klansman dressed in red shouted, "Aliens of the outer world! Now you are candidates for naturalization as citizens of the Invisible Empire, Knights of the Ku Klux Klan. If there is one among you who in his heart of hearts knows that he harbors some ulterior motive and will not remain loyal to all the obligations and duties of the Ku Klux Klan, then I command you to step aside and go no further." No one spoke or moved. "Have you shown yourselves at all times to be loyal to true Americanism, Protestant Christianity, and white supremacy?" the red Klansman went on.

There was a murmur of voices that sounded like "Yes, we have." With a nod from the Klansman in blue, the men began to circle the burning cross, with their right hands raised in some kind of salute. They were saying something, but I couldn't make out what it was. Finally, after two circles, they returned to their column formation in front of the three Klansmen leaders.

Then the Klansman in purple stepped forth. "Candidates, kneel!" he shouted. Suddenly my heart was in my throat, because I recognized that voice. I glanced over at Joshua to see if he had too, but there was nothing in his face that told me he knew what I had just discovered. My heart was racing, but I forced myself to turn back to look just as the white-robed Klansmen got down on their knees. "Do you solemnly swear that you'll always be faithful to our God and his son, Jesus Christ, and to the only true religion, Christianity?"

"We do!" the men on their knees shouted.

I watched their movement stir up some of the dust. I was sure now that I had been right about the man in the purple robe and hood.

"Do you believe that the United States is a white man's country and that it should always remain a white man's country?"

"We do!"

"Will you do all in your power to uphold the principles of white supremacy and the purity of white womanhood?"

"We will!"

"By the authority vested in me as the imperial wizard, Knights of the Ku Klux Klan, I dub you Klansmen, the most honored title among men!"

The ceremony seemed to be over, and the Klansmen who had been kneeling returned to their respective corners of the pasture. I thought maybe Joshua had been wrong about the Klan punishing Theodore, but then two Klansmen emerged from the shadows. Each of them was holding a rope tied to one wrist of a tall, lanky Negro man. "Is that Theodore?" I asked Joshua in a whisper.

He nodded.

The two Klansmen handed Theodore over to the red- and blue-robed Klansmen and disappeared behind the burning cross. Each of them took one of the ropes, and they began pulling in opposite directions until Theodore's arms were perpendicular to his body. I was sure if they pulled harder his arms would come out of their sockets. The imperial wizard produced a whip from behind his back, stepped forward, and began lashing Theodore. I cringed in expectation of Theodore's cries, but there was nothing except the sound of the whip as it sliced through his skin. I felt sick and desperately wanted to leave, but I couldn't move.

Slowly Theodore began to sink toward the ground, but the red- and blue-robed Klansmen kept the ropes taut until the imperial wizard stopped. Then they let go of the ropes, and Theodore fell the rest of the way, disappearing from our view.

Suddenly someone grabbed my neck, and I twisted around

to see a white-hooded Klansman looking down at me. "Run, Woodrow!" Joshua shouted.

I kicked at the hem of the Klansman's robe. He let out a yelp and let go of my neck. I jumped to my feet and raced down the creek bank. I heard shouts behind me as I tore through the bushes and trees toward Squaw Creek. I hadn't known I could run so fast. I was almost certain the shouts were fading, but I didn't stop. I kept running and running until I saw lights to my left, so I headed in that direction. Before long, I was behind some houses. I stopped and bent over, trying to catch my breath. I hoped I might hear Joshua coming along the bank behind me, but there was no sound except the barking of dogs in the backyards of some of the houses. I waited a few more minutes. If Joshua had been behind me, I was sure he'd have caught up with me by now—he knew the terrain much better than I did. Could he have taken off in a different direction? Or was he already way ahead of me?

When I finally reached our house, I checked the attic to see if Joshua was there, but he wasn't. I left the front door unlocked for him in case he eventually showed up.

As I headed down the hallway to my room, I was once again drawn to the window at the end of the hall. I stood there looking at the house next door, waiting, until finally I saw the Buick Touring pull into the driveway. But Senator Crawford didn't drive on into the garage. Instead, he got out of the automobile and looked straight up at my window. I was sure he couldn't see me, but there was absolutely no doubt in my mind that the imperial wizard of the Ku Klux Klan knew I had seen him tonight.

chapter TEN

I slept, but I dreamed, and in my dreams I was being chased by hooded men with whips. I kept shouting to them that I was white and almost like a son to Senator Crawford, but that didn't seem to make any difference. Then, just when I thought I had outrun them, I fell into Squaw Creek, but instead of being only a trickle, it was a torrent, and several times I thought I would be swept downstream and drown. But at the last moment, I was able to grab hold of an exposed root and pull myself to safety just before the hooded men reached me.

When I finally awakened, I was shivering uncontrollably and was drenched in sweat. My room was that grayish color of just before dawn, and even though I was so tired that I found it hard to keep my eyes open, I didn't want to go back to sleep because I knew the hooded men would be waiting for me. I just lay there waiting for morning to come so I could to talk to Senator Crawford. I desperately wanted to believe he could explain what I had seen the night before.

I stood up unsteadily, stripped off my pajamas, and dried myself with my blanket. When I was dressed I checked the attic again to see if Joshua had come in after I had gone to bed, but he still wasn't there.

As I headed downstairs, I smelled something burning, and when I got to the kitchen I saw smoke coming from the toaster. "Mary!" My shout brought her back from whatever she had been thinking about and she quickly unplugged it. "What's wrong?" I asked.

When Mary didn't reply, I started to repeat my question, but just as I opened my mouth, she asked, "Do you know where Joshua is?"

Her question startled me so much I almost said, "I haven't seen him since last night," but I caught myself and said, "I thought he was in Chicago. Did he come back home?"

Mary mumbled something like, "I don't think he's really happy there."

Now there was more smoke coming from the stove, and I

realized that the bacon was also burning. Mary turned out the flame and then looked at me. I could see both fear and anger in her eyes. It almost made me tell her what had happened last night, but I didn't think I could without revealing Senator Crawford's secret, so I just said, "Don't worry. Joshua can take care of himself." Maybe now he really *was* on his way to Chicago. Mary gave me a puzzled look, and I could tell that she wanted to say something else, but I cut her off with "I'm really not very hungry now. I'll eat something later."

I went upstairs, opened Mama's bedroom door, and looked inside. She was sitting up in bed. "Hello, Woodrow," she said softly.

"How are you feeling, Mama?"

"I took something to help me sleep last night, so my head is a little fuzzy this morning, but other than that I'm all right."

"I think I'll go over to Senator Crawford's house," I said.

"Why?" Mama asked.

"Because he needs me."

Mama coughed. "Oh, Woodrow, you can be so naive sometimes. How can a perfect stranger need you?"

"Because he doesn't have a son anymore, and I don't have a father. I'm not being *naive*, Mama. Senator Crawford said he'd teach me how to paint, and he wants to take me fishing, and he wants to do all kinds of things that he would do with Robert if he were still alive." I couldn't tell her that I also needed to understand why someone I liked so much could have done something that seemed so wrong.

Just then Mary came into the room, grabbed me by the arm, and pulled me out into the hallway. "You mustn't upset your mama, Mr. Woodrow. You have to remember that—"

I didn't let her finish. I ran out of the house and down the front steps, across the lawn, and up onto Senator Crawford's front porch. Benjamin opened the door and let me inside. "Senator Crawford is in the solarium, Mr. Woodrow," he said. "He asked me to tell you when you got here to go back there."

"How did he know I was coming?"

Benjamin just looked at me for a moment, then he said, "I'll get you a glass of lemonade, Mr. Woodrow."

I remained where I was until Benjamin returned with the lemonade, wondering what I was going to say to Senator Crawford when I saw him, and wondering too if he was going to say anything to me about what happened last night. "You'd better go on in," Benjamin said.

I took a sip of the lemonade and enjoyed the sensation the cold tartness made on its way to my stomach. "All right."

Senator Crawford was sitting on his stool, behind his easel, his head close to the canvas. "Come closer, Woodrow. I'm very pleased with today's effort, and I really do want your opinion. Some days, everything just comes together creatively, and this is one of those days, because this morning I've felt almost as, I'm sure, God felt when he created this delicate flower so long ago." He lifted his brush from the canvas, regarded the flower for a moment, then laid the brush down and finally looked at me. "What do you think?"

I walked up to the painting. Senator Crawford was right. It looked exactly like the flower in a vase on the table beside him. "I wish I could do that," I said.

"It takes a very steady hand, and this morning my hands are very steady." Now he turned and looked directly at me. "Would you like to know why?"

"Why?"

"I was angry yesterday, but I'm no longer angry today, and I think that's the secret. I was able to get rid of that anger, and now, this morning, I can create this masterpiece." He paused and then asked me, "How is your mother?"

"I don't know. Some days I think she's all right, then other days I don't. We had an argument today."

"What was it about?"

"You."

A hint of a smile rippled along Senator Crawford's lips, but it didn't settle in permanently, and he clasped his hands together and made a steeple with his two index fingers, which he then placed below his nostrils. "Is that right?" I nodded. "Well, I'd like to hear about it," he said.

"It all started when I told Mama I was coming over here, and she asked me why."

"What did you give her as a reason?"

"I told her that you didn't have a son anymore, and that I didn't have a father." I felt myself choking up. "It's true."

"Come here, Woodrow," Senator Crawford said. I moved closer to him. "Do you want to tell me anything else?" I actually felt my heart skip a beat and I was surer he knew I had seen what happened in the pasture. When I didn't say anything, Senator Crawford asked, "Well, do you?"

Without looking at him, I said, "Yes, sir." With that admission, I realized that this was going to be easier than I had thought it would be. And I was relieved to be talking to him about it now. I told myself that Joshua really *was* on his way to Chicago this time, so I wasn't betraying his trust. No one could hurt him now, so I didn't have to lie to Senator Crawford about anything that had happened. "Last night, I went with Joshua to the Klan meeting."

"I thought Joshua was in Chicago," Senator Crawford said.

"He wasn't. He was living with other people, except last night, when he planned to sleep in our attic."

"And you honestly didn't know where he was until last night?"

I shook my head. "No, sir."

"That means Mary was lying to you, doesn't it?"

"Yes, sir."

"What did you think about what you saw last night, Woodrow?"

"It really upset me."

My answer seemed to disappoint him. For a couple of minutes, he just stared at me, then he said, "Well, tell me why you went there with Joshua in the first place."

"He told me that his friend Theodore was going to be punished for something he did, and he wanted me to go with him to see it happen."

"Did you go because you believe the Klan shouldn't be doing things like that to Negroes?"

I shrugged. "I didn't know what the Klan was going to do. But if a person does something wrong, then I guess he should be punished. But I didn't think that—"

Senator Crawford stood up. "It's that, but it's also much,

much more," he said, interrupting me. "It's the pollution of the white race, which goes against what God intended or he wouldn't have made us the way we are. The white man is superior to other races, and he always will be, and we go against God's will if we pollute our race by allowing a Negro man and a white woman to marry." When I didn't say anything, Senator Crawford continued. "So that's why we had to punish Theodore last night, Woodrow, punish him severely enough that he and other Negro men in town would never again do what he did. He was flirting with a good white Christian girl, because he had evil thoughts in his head and in his heart, and if we don't stop this sort of thing now, it'll be impossible to stop it later." Senator Crawford sat back down on his stool. "I need to finish this last petal," he said. He was breathing hard, and his face was flushed. "Sit here beside me, and together, let's see if we can even come close to creating what God has already done so perfectly."

I set my glass of lemonade down on the floor and joined him at my easel. I began sketching the outline of the orchid onto my canvas, but my brain was still trying to make sense of what Senator Crawford had told me. What he said happened with Theodore and the white girl sounded much worse than what Joshua said happened. Who was telling the truth?

For the next several minutes, Senator Crawford and I sat together in silence, painstakingly trying to create the perfect orchid—like God did, Senator Crawford kept saying, sometimes out loud, sometimes in a whisper—until he finally said, "I've done the best I can do, Woodrow. Would you care to look at it again and tell me what you think?"

I got up off my stool and walked around behind him to get a better look, and once again I was in awe of what I saw. "It's beautiful. It looks so real. I don't think I'll ever be able to do that."

"Oh yes, you too shall be able to create your own masterpiece one of these days, but you have to work hard to reach that stage of perfection. You must never give up on yourself, and you must never believe that you are incapable of perfection." He paused and smiled. "What did you think last night when you realized that I was the imperial wizard?" he asked.

I took a deep breath and let it out. "I was disappointed, I guess."

But I wasn't sure Senator Crawford was even listening, because he said, "Come with me, Woodrow. I want to show you something."

I followed him out of the solarium and back into the house. In his bedroom, there was an old free-standing wardrobe, which he said his grandfather had built in Pennsylvania and which his father had moved to Mississippi and which he himself finally had moved to Oklahoma. He took a large skeleton key out of his pocket, inserted it into the lock, and opened the door. Inside there were robes and hoods of all different colors. He took out the purple one and put it on. After he adjusted the hood so he could see through the slits, he looked directly at me and said, "I am the imperial wizard of the Knights of the Ku Klux Klan, and I have the power of life and death over the Negroes and the Catholics and the Jews and the criminals who want to destroy our white civilization, and you, Woodrow Harper, must join me in the battle to make sure that this never happens."

For just a moment, I didn't think I had heard him correctly. Finally I managed to say, "*Me?*"

Senator Crawford nodded. "But you must never tell anyone about this, *not even your mother*, unless I say you can, because only a chosen few know who I am."

I found that hard to believe, because the minute I had heard his voice the night before, I'd known it was him in the purple robe and hood, but I didn't say anything.

Senator Crawford removed his hood. "I want to show you something else, Woodrow." He pushed back the other robes in the wardrobe, revealing a smaller purple robe and hood.

"Let's try these on for size." Senator Crawford opened the robe, and I put my arms through the sleeves, and then he fastened it for me.

"It fits," I said.

"It belonged to Robert, and he was so proud of it, Woodrow. Now let's put on the hood."

Senator Crawford placed the hood on my head, adjusted it so that I could see through the slits, and then he stepped back. "I like what I see, Woodrow! I want you to go with me to the next monthly meeting of the Klan, and I want you to wear this. Will you do that for me?" When I hesitated, Senator Crawford frowned and asked, "What's wrong?"

"What will you want me to do?" I asked. "Will you be whipping someone else?" I took a deep breath and let it out. "I don't think I could ever do anything like that. It's just not right."

Senator Crawford put a hand on my shoulder. "Oh, Woodrow, stop thinking so much about what you saw last night. That's not what the Klan does unless it's really necessary."

"All right," I said. "I'll go then, if I don't have to whip anyone." Even saying the words made my stomach clench.

Senator Crawford gave me a big smile. "You just need to trust me more, Woodrow."

chapter ELEVEN

As I headed back to my house, an idea that had started to form when Senator Crawford announced he wanted me to go with him to the next Klan meeting became clearer. If I became a member of the Klan, I could work from the inside to make the Klan the way Winifred had described it to Mama and me on our first day here. We'd get rid of crime in Lawton and make it a better place to live, but we'd stop doing terrible things to Negroes. People would listen to me because I had been chosen by Senator Crawford and he was one of the most important men in the state. I wanted to go on painting with Senator Crawford and talking with him about all the things I'd never been able to discuss with my own father.

But the man who treated me like a son, who wanted to take me fishing and searching for buried treasure in the mountains, couldn't continue to do what I'd seen him do to Theodore. I had to convince him to change.

That night I slept better than I had in weeks.

The day after Labor Day, Mama drove us to school and dropped me off at the seventh-grade end of the building. Jimmy showed me around the building and introduced me to all his friends. He told me he'd spent the last few weeks at a church camp in the Arbuckle Mountains, east of Lawton, and that he wasn't angry with me at all. I was sorry he and I didn't have any classes together, but every day at lunch, I sat with him and his friends in the cafeteria. I felt that his friends were becoming my friends too.

On Saturday I'd finished my homework by noon and was wondering how to spend the rest of the day when Mary appeared at my door to tell me Jimmy was on the phone and wanted to talk to me.

"You need to come to church tomorrow, Woodrow," Jimmy said without any other greeting. "The preacher's sermon is based on a verse from Deuteronomy."

"All right. What church do you go to?"

"*God's* church, of course. Your mother should come too."

"I'll ask her, but she's a Presbyterian, so she might not want to go," I told him.

"That's too bad, because in Lawton it's very important that you go to the *right* church so you'll know what the Lord wants from you for the rest of the week."

"I can go by myself."

"You can go with Senator Crawford, but he's one of our deacons, so he has to be there early. You'll need to be ready to leave tomorrow morning at eight o'clock."

"I'll be ready."

When I got back upstairs, I went to Mama's room and took the Westclox from her night table. I set the alarm for 7:00 a.m.

The next morning I put on my best clothes—a white shirt, a blue suit, a lighter blue tie, and black shoes—and went over to Senator Crawford's house. Mama was still asleep, so I left her a note so she wouldn't worry.

Benjamin opened the door. "I'm going to church with Senator Crawford," I told him.

"You look very nice, Mr. Woodrow. Just have a seat, and I'll tell Senator Crawford you're here."

I sat down stiffly on a chair in the living room. It had been almost a year since I had worn this suit, and now it felt a little tight.

"Woodrow!"

Senator Crawford was standing in the doorway. I stood up and walked over to him. "I want to go to church with you." I supposed that I should have told him Jimmy suggested it, but I suddenly wanted him to think it was my idea.

"I was hoping you would one of these days, but I didn't want to say anything about it before you were ready," Senator Crawford said. "I'll be proud for you to go to church with me."

We left his house together, both of us dressed in blue suits, with black shoes and ties that almost matched, and I felt even more that I was where I belonged. When we got to the church, Senator Crawford introduced me to a lot of people, whose names I forgot almost immediately, and they all greeted me warmly. I could tell by the look on Senator Crawford's face that he was proud of me.

Mrs. Kennard, who was the wife of Lawton's mayor, took me to my Sunday school class. Jimmy was sitting in one of the wooden chairs at the front of the room. He looked up and smiled. It wasn't long before the classroom started to fill up with other boys and girls. Most of them I had met at Medicine Park or at school, but some of them Jimmy had to introduce to me. They all seemed really friendly and happy that I was there with them.

When it was time for Sunday school to begin, a man came in and announced that Mrs. Powell, our teacher, was ill and that Jimmy would take over for her. Jimmy must have known this was going to happen, because he didn't act surprised. He talked for almost an hour, quoting verses from the Bible, pounding his fist on the pulpit to make a point, and causing me to flinch a couple of times. But by the time he finished, I didn't feel the same way I had felt when I got to church that morning. I felt that something had really happened to me, just like Jimmy told me I would. When I told him that, as the two of us headed to the church sanctuary, he said matter-of-factly, "It's the Holy Spirit working within you, Woodrow."

The sanctuary was almost full when we got there. "Where are we going to sit?" I asked.

"I'm sure Senator Crawford will want you to sit with him," Jimmy said. "He always sits in the fifth pew. There are three places there that nobody else ever uses, one for him, one for his wife, and one for Robert."

"Why?" I asked before I could stop myself. "They're both dead."

"They'll always be with us in spirit, Woodrow. You'll sit next to him, where Robert would be sitting if he were alive."

Jimmy showed me to Senator Crawford's pew, which I could have found on my own because of all the people standing around it, waiting their turn to talk to him. When Senator Crawford saw me, he stopped talking and greeted me with a big smile. Everyone standing around him smiled too. Senator Crawford wanted me to be there, and there was nowhere else I wanted to be at that moment.

Senator Crawford introduced me to Mayor Kennard, who said, "We're all united behind Senator Crawford, Woodrow, because we all want the same three things for Lawton: strict control of criminal activity, the end of corruption in local government, and the moral purification of the town. We're glad that you've joined us."

I listened as politely as I could while Mayor Kennard gave a short speech about all of his accomplishments since he had been in office. Finally somebody began playing the piano, and the people around us went to their own pews. For the next thirty minutes, we sang songs and prayed, and then Reverend Clark walked up to the pulpit. I hadn't met him today, but he looked familiar, and I thought I had seen him in the dining room of the Apache Inn in Medicine Park.

"We have been told a lie for almost two thousand years," Reverend Clark began. "It is so ingrained in our psyche that the Jews are God's chosen people and that the Bible is the history of the Jews and that we Gentiles can somehow be a part of all of this if we do certain things. But, people, how can the Jews be the chosen people of God and how can we Gentiles come to Christ through people who are the antichrist?"

There were several "Amens!" from people all over the sanctuary, which startled me, but nobody else seemed to notice.

"If you trace the promises that God made to Abraham, it will most certainly lead you not to the Jews but to the true Israelites—the Aryan people—all of whom were originally white until miscegenation, the mixing of the races, set in," Reverend Clark continued. "Fortunately for the world, there are still some of us who are of that original pure white stock." Reverend Clark stopped and looked out over the congregation. "Miscegenation is an act that God has warned us about many, many times, my good fellow Christians!" Reverend Clark shouted, pounding his fist so hard on the pulpit that I was sure he had cracked the wood. "In Deuteronomy chapter twenty-three, verse two, you'll find the law that Moses laid down to Israel. 'A bastard shall not enter into the congregation of the Lord, even to his tenth generation shall he not enter into the congregation of the Lord!'" Reverend Clark closed his eyes. "People, it can't be clearer than that!"

Several people, including Senator Crawford, shouted, "Amen."

"Let us pray," Reverend Clark said. For a long time, he prayed, and even though I tried to focus on his words, I was more amazed by the fact that he could talk for that long about anything. When Reverend Clark finished praying, he said, "Our invitational hymn is on page forty, and we're going to sing five verses as we wait to see who the Holy Spirit has moved to come down this center aisle today."

The pianist played a short introduction, and I had just found page forty in my hymnal when I felt Senator Crawford's hand on my shoulder. I looked over at him and then I saw Jimmy standing at the end of the pew, one hand outstretched, motioning me to come with him, so I squeezed past Senator Crawford and joined Jimmy in the aisle. Together we walked to the front of the sanctuary, which seemed like a very long trip, and were greeted by Reverend Clark, who put his hands on my head and started praying again. It was hard to hear what he was saying because of the singing of the hymn, but I was able to pick out a few words here and there to get the gist of it. It was all about how now that I had let Jesus come into my heart, I would be saved from spending an eternity in hell.

I was the only one who came forward that morning, even after *six* verses—we sang an extra one for the person who Reverend Clark said he was sure was feeling a tug at his heartstrings, but whoever it was must have decided to wait for another day. Jimmy took me immediately out of the sanctuary and ushered me up some stairs and into a little room, where he told me to take off my clothes. "Why?" I said.

"You're going to be baptized, Woodrow. You're going to have your sins washed away."

"I don't know what *sins* you're talking about, Jimmy." Away from the hymns and the preaching, I felt less sure about what I was doing. How had things gone this far?

Jimmy smiled. "Well, God knows, even if you don't."

Everything was happening so fast that I was beginning to feel out of control. Did I really want to do this? But then I thought of how proud Senator Crawford had been introducing me to everyone at church, and how he'd wanted me to sit next to him, in Robert's place, in his pew. The memory of that horrible scene in the pasture was starting to seem like something I'd made up, much less real than the happy times I'd spent with Senator Crawford at his house.

I slipped into the white robe that Jimmy handed me, then he went over and opened a little door, and I could see a small rectangular pool of water. Reverend Clark was standing in the middle of it.

"This is called the baptistry," Jimmy said. "It's supposed to be the River Jordan, because that's where John the Baptist baptized Jesus." Reverend Clark was smiling and holding out his hand to me. "Be careful going down the steps, Woodrow," Jimmy whispered to me. "They're slippery."

Slowly, I started down the steps, feeling the wet concrete under my feet, until I touched Reverend Clark's hand, and he led me to the center of the baptistry. "Senator Crawford is so proud of you, Woodrow," Reverend Clark whispered. "So is Jesus." I nodded. I was suddenly scared to death. "Now, I'm going to say a few words to the congregation, then I'm going to hold your nose and dunk you under the water," Reverend Clark whispered. "Don't open your mouth, all right?"

"All right," I whispered back.

"My fellow Christians, Woodrow Harper has confessed his sins and has let Jesus come into his heart," Reverend Clark said to the congregation. "As the apostle Peter said in Acts chapter two, verse thirty-eight, 'Repent, and let every one of you be baptized in the name of Jesus Christ for the remission of sins;

and you shall receive the gift of the Holy Spirit.'" With that, Reverend Clark dunked me in the water, but I was back up so fast that I didn't really realize what had happened. "God bless you, Woodrow," Reverend Clark said as he gently guided me back toward the steps, where I saw Jimmy waiting for me in the little room with a big white towel. I removed the wet robe, dried off, and then got dressed again.

"Now you're a pure white Christian, Woodrow," Jimmy said, "and it's up to you to help us spread God's word about what that means. Are you ready to do it?" But before I could ask Jimmy exactly what it was I'd be expected to do, he added, "Senator Crawford will want you to come with him to our house for Sunday dinner."

I'd left home without any breakfast, and I suddenly realized how hungry I was. I decided that any questions I had could wait until after we ate.

chapter TWELVE

Senator Crawford put his arm around my shoulders as we headed down the church steps. I noticed that all the other boys—including Jimmy—were walking with their fathers in the same way. The girls were following behind with their mothers, and I could hear them talking about what they were going to serve for Sunday dinner. It felt good to finally feel as if I belonged.

"Did you understand Reverend Clark's sermon, Woodrow?" Senator Crawford asked as we crossed C Avenue to where he had parked his automobile along the curb.

"Yes, sir, I think I did."

"Well, Reverend Clark knows how to wring the truth from

the Bible, something I can't say for all preachers, that's for certain. When Reverend Clark is preaching, always listen carefully, Woodrow, because he is God's anointed messenger, a vessel of the Holy Spirit, and it's the same as if God himself had just sent Reverend Clark a telegram from heaven."

I suddenly had an image of a long line of telegraph poles with humming wires strung from Lawton up into the sky, all the way to heaven, bringing sermons directly to Reverend Clark each Sunday morning. As we headed down Sixth Street to the Joneses' house, I kept imagining the telegraph lines and thinking about God sending sermons to Reverend Clark.

When we got to the Joneses' house, I saw several automobiles parked in front and on the side streets. "I didn't know so many people would be here," I told Senator Crawford.

"Oh yes, Woodrow, there's a big group of us here in Lawton who meet every Sunday after church to have dinner together and discuss what we need to do to keep Lawton safe for pure white Christians. If it weren't for the decisions we make each Sunday, I'm afraid it wouldn't be long until the heathens took over, and that's not what God has in mind."

I wanted to ask him why Lawton shouldn't be safe for Mary and Joshua too, but right then he turned into the only empty parking place in front of the Joneses' house and expertly parked the Buick Touring in it. So all I said was, "We were lucky."

"No, Woodrow, a spot is always saved for me, no matter where we're meeting. It's a sign of respect."

We got out and headed up the steps to Jimmy's front porch. Mrs. Jones opened the door before we could ring the bell. "Hello, Senator! Hello, Woodrow! I'll call everyone to dinner now that you're here, so you can say the blessing." Actually, she didn't have to say anything, because as soon as the people who were sitting in the living room saw us, they all rose and followed her into the dining room.

Jimmy came up to me and said, "We eat in the kitchen, so the grown-ups can talk. I'm hungry, aren't you? You'll love Wilma's pot roast. She's the best cook in Comanche County, I can tell you that, and she's been with us forever."

I followed Jimmy through a swinging door into the kitchen. There was an older Negro woman and a younger Negro woman standing at the stove, stirring things and looking into the oven. The other boys and girls, whom I recognized from Sunday school, were already sitting around the table, but the chair at the head and a corner chair next to it were vacant. When I started to sit in the corner chair, Jimmy grabbed my arm, and said, "No, Woodrow, you sit at the head."

So I sat there, knowing that because I was with Senator Crawford I was special, even in somebody else's house. "Hi," I said to everyone.

"Hello, Woodrow," they all said in unison.

"Lizzy, we're going to say the blessing now," Jimmy said to the younger Negro woman, "and when we're through, you may serve us."

"Yes, sir, Mr. Jimmy," Lizzy said without looking our way.

Jimmy's blessing was about the food that was going to be set before us, and about being ever mindful of who we were— pure white Christian people—and about the races always being kept separate, so that the white race would never be polluted by the coloreds. I snuck a look toward the stove, where Wilma and Lizzy continued to work quietly. I wondered if they were paying attention to what Jimmy was saying, knowing that they couldn't help hearing him. Finally Jimmy said, "Amen!" and the others joined in with their amens.

I knew that Lizzy at least must have been *listening*, even if she hadn't been paying attention, because as soon as Jimmy stopped, she turned and brought to the table a large platter of pot roast surrounded by potatoes, carrots, squash, and white onions. She followed that with a huge basket of dinner rolls and a bowl of brown gravy. No one said anything until after Lizzy had served us. I had never been in such a formal setting with other people my age, and I felt a little uncomfortable, as though if I picked up the wrong utensil, I would be asked to leave the table.

"This looks so good," Betty Archer said. In a lower voice she added, "I was glad it was your family's turn to have dinner, because our nigra can't cook pot roast worth a hill of beans."

I took a bite of the pot roast and it almost melted in my mouth. "It's excellent, Jimmy," I told him. Jimmy passed me the gravy and I ladled some over my potatoes. I had never tasted anything as wonderful as that either.

For several minutes we mostly just ate, but from time to time somebody said something about a particular Bible verse or section of Reverend Clark's sermon. I had hoped we'd talk about school or what they did for fun in Lawton, but instead Jimmy said, "I've made a list of the people we need to witness to this week, and I'll give each one of you a copy of it before you leave." I started to ask Jimmy what he meant by that, but before I could, Lizzy served us banana pudding, and it was so delicious I forgot about everything else.

When Lizzy finally cleared the table, Jimmy stood up, said, "I'll be back in a couple of minutes," and left the room.

Betty smiled at me. "We're so glad you moved to Lawton, Woodrow," she said.

"Thank you," I said. I started telling them about my life in Washington but after a couple of minutes, I realized that nobody was paying attention to me. Their eyes were glued to the door, waiting for Jimmy to return. When he finally came back, he had several sheets of paper in his hand. He gave one to each of us. "What does witnessing mean?" I asked. "Do we read the Bible to them?"

Jimmy smiled, but it was a crooked smile, and there was a look in his eyes that scared me. "No, Woodrow, it's a little early yet for true *Christian* witnessing."

Everyone at the table laughed.

"Then how *do* we witness to them?"

"We ride our bicycles by their houses and call them 'nigger lovers,'" Billy Wallace said. "After a while they come outside to confront us, but we're too strong for them because God is on our side, and they know that in their hearts, so in the end they just stand there and take their punishment."

"There are boys and girls in our school who don't just need to have their sins washed away, Woodrow, they're ready for a good scrubbing," Jimmy said. "They're all nigger lovers. They talk to niggers, they invite niggers into their homes, and they think niggers are just as good as white people."

I didn't ever remember hearing that word used so many

times, and I could almost see a physical change taking place in Jimmy's face as he spoke.

"If we don't do this, Woodrow, then our white blood will become tainted," Douglas Rogers said, "and we'll no longer be the superior race God meant us to be."

"We need to make nigger lovers pure again, Woodrow," Betty said. "We need to show them the error of their ways."

"Well, what happens after we've done this?"

"Why are you asking so many questions, Woodrow?" Billy said. "Do you have a problem with what we're doing?"

"No, Billy." I managed to smile. "I just want to make sure I understand what it is that will be required of me."

"Most of the time, they stop treating niggers as though they were the equals of white people," Jimmy said.

"How do you know that?" I asked.

"Oh, we know," Billy said. "In a town like Lawton, it's easy to find out such things."

"If you're a nigger lover in Lawton," Jimmy said, "then we'll find out who you are."

My mind was racing. Why had I thought I could avoid doing anything like this before I could start changing the Klan? But how could I get out of it without their thinking that I was a nigger lover, *just like Daddy*? When he was growing up, had boys and girls ridden their bikes past *his* house, calling him names? I wondered. Was this what Mama had meant when she talked about the difficult times Daddy had had growing up in Lawton?

I pushed the thoughts aside. Daddy wasn't here, and I needed to deal with the boys and girls who were looking expectantly at me now. *It's only a word,* I told myself. It had been said so many times at the dinner table that I hardly noticed it anymore. I'd go witnessing with the others, and then I'd try to forget what I'd done and concentrate on changing things so Senator Crawford and I could go fishing and paint wildflowers out in the mountains.

"Woodrow?"

I looked up and saw Senator Crawford standing at the door to the kitchen. "Yes, sir?"

"It's getting late. We need to leave."

I stood up so suddenly that I knocked over my chair, and everyone at the table gave me a strange look. "I'm sorry," I said. As I bent down to pick it up, I knew my face was bright red. I hoped they would all think I was only embarrassed because I had knocked over the chair, and not that it had happened because I could hardly wait to get out of there. When I straightened up, I looked at Jimmy and said, "I'll be ready whenever you are!"

For just a moment, I thought I saw a glint of something in his eyes before he smiled and said, "Do you have a bicycle?"

"Yes."

"Good." Jimmy stood up and shook my hand, to seal some sort of pact, I guessed. "One day this week I'll ride over to your house after school, and we'll do our witnessing together."

"All right," I said.

"God bless you, Woodrow," Douglas and Billy said in unison.

"The war that Jesus Christ wants us to wage against the infidels is unstoppable," Jimmy said, "and we're all happy that you are one of his Christian soldiers."

Out of the corner of my eye, I saw Senator Crawford smile and nod his head. I wanted him to approve of me as much as he approved of Jimmy, so I saluted Jimmy and said, "Woodrow Harper, Christian soldier, reporting for duty, sir!" That seemed to take everyone by surprise, but then they all applauded, including Senator Crawford, and I knew that I too had done something that Senator Crawford was proud of. As we left the kitchen, I started to compliment Wilma and Lizzy on the wonderful food, but Senator Crawford's left hand was guiding me toward the living room.

I told both Mr. and Mrs. Jones how much I had enjoyed the meal, their hospitality, and the Christian fellowship, trying to remember as much as I could from Jimmy's earlier blessing, and it really seemed to please them. Mr. Jones even clapped Senator Crawford on the back and said, "You have a fine young man there, George, a fine young man."

"I know," Senator Crawford said. "I'm proud of him."

"You should be," Mrs. Jones said.

We told everyone else good-bye, and as we were going out the front door I realized that nobody had left, because everyone had to stay until after Senator Crawford was gone. As we headed down the steps toward Senator Crawford's automobile, it made me feel good to know that. The closer we got to my house, though, the more my stomach felt funny. How was I going to explain to Mama what had happened to me today? I turned to look at Senator Crawford and saw that he was watching me. "It's time for you to tell her, Woodrow," he said in a soft voice. "She needs to know *everything*."

"*Everything?*"

Senator Crawford nodded. "Yes, everything, because there's nothing to be ashamed of. You'll tell her that the way you feel now is the way every good white Christian should feel." He slowed down to turn into his driveway. "I love you just like a son, Woodrow. You should always remember that."

"I will. I promise."

When I got out of the Buick Touring, I noticed Winifred's automobile parked in our driveway, and I was glad that I wouldn't have to face Mama alone. I stopped just inside, suddenly realizing that whenever I came into this house from being with Senator Crawford, I always felt a little guilty about what I had said and done. I heard Mary moving around in the kitchen and decided to go there first. I stood in the doorway for a few minutes without saying anything, watching Mary as she dried a plate, then I said, "Have you heard from Joshua yet?"

Mary dropped the plate, and it shattered into at least a hundred pieces. She turned around and looked at me. "You shouldn't sneak up on people like that, Mr. Woodrow, because there's not much left of your grandma Harper's good china, and now your mama will probably be upset with me because of what I just did."

"I'll tell her it was my fault, Mary."

"Nothing is ever white folks' fault, Mr. Woodrow. Nothing."

I turned to leave, but then I realized that Mary hadn't answered my question about Joshua, so I repeated it. Mary shook her head. "He'll call you soon," I told her. "I know he will, just as soon as he . . . can," I added. I could tell that Mary wanted to ask me some questions about Joshua, but there was still no way I was going to let her know anything about what we had done. "I saw Winifred's automobile parked in our driveway," I said. "What's she doing here?"

Mary nodded. "She and your mama are visiting in the sitting room."

"I'll go say hello to them."

Mama and Winifred were sitting in a couple of wing chairs around a small table. As soon as Mama saw me, she stood up. "Where have you been, Woodrow?"

I went into the room before I said anything. "At church. I left you a note. You were asleep when I left, and I didn't want to wake you up."

"What church?"

"*God's* church. I went with Senator Crawford. The mayor of Lawton goes there too, and so do all of my friends."

"I don't know anything about this church, Woodrow," Mama said.

I looked at her. "I didn't think you would care. You've never once mentioned going to church since we've been in Lawton."

"Church has been over for a while, Woodrow. What have you been doing in the meantime?"

"We went to dinner at the Joneses' house, because we needed to talk about some things we're going to do."

"What kind of things?"

Senator Crawford had said to tell Mama everything, but I couldn't bring myself to do it, because now it sounded so awful. "Just stuff that the kids do, Mama," I said. "I want to belong, that's all, and Jimmy and his friends are the most important kids in school. It's not easy always being an outsider. Senator Crawford is really happy about what I'm doing, and that's important to me too."

"I will not let you go to church with a member of the Ku Klux Klan!" Mama shouted. "Don't you have any idea what those people are? Woodrow, they stand for all the things that your father fought against!"

"Peggy! Peggy! Calm down," Winifred said. She took hold of Mama's arm. "I told you, sweetheart, the Klan here in Lawton isn't like the Klan elsewhere. It only wants to—"

"How did you know Senator Crawford was a member of the Ku Klux Klan?" I interrupted her to ask Mama. "It's supposed to be a secret."

"It's no secret, Woodrow," Mama said. "It seems that everyone knows what he is . . . including Mary!"

"Peggy, you're getting yourself all upset about nothing," Winifred said.

"*Nothing?* Winifred, I think you and the rest of the people in this town need to open your eyes to what's really going on here!"

"Senator Crawford is a wonderful man, Mama! He only wants to help us!" I shouted at her. "He treats me like his son. And that's more than Daddy ever did! And I have a plan that'll make everything all right!"

I turned to run out of the room, but Mary was blocking the way, and her dark eyes were boring into me. "You and I have to talk," she said firmly.

chapter THIRTEEN

As we followed Mary into the kitchen, Mama said, "It was a mistake to come back here, Winifred. This town is full of people I just don't know how to deal with."

Mama and I sat down at our usual places at the kitchen table, and Winifred sat down opposite Mama. Mama told Mary to make some coffee and to pour me a glass of milk. I knew both Mama and Winifred were staring at me, but I couldn't look at them.

I used a finger to trace the patterns of the wood on the tabletop, pretending they were roads that would take me anywhere but where I was at that moment. I was wishing I hadn't mentioned that I had a plan, because I realized how foolish—

how *naive*—it would sound if I tried to explain it. And how could they possibly understand how much I needed Senator Crawford to be a father to me? If he really wanted me to fill the emptiness that Robert's death had left in his life—and I believed with all my heart that he did—I was sure I could change him.

Finally the coffee was ready. "Pour yourself a cup too, Mary," Mama said, "and then sit down here with us."

I wondered what Jimmy would think if he showed up now and saw Mary sitting at our kitchen table. I felt my stomach clench. I had finally thought of a way I could fit in in Lawton, and I was afraid Mama was about to destroy it by treating our Negro housekeeper like a member of our family.

After a while, when no one had uttered a single word, I said, "All right, Mary, what do you want to know?"

"Where's Joshua?"

"Well, he didn't go to Chicago, like you said," I replied. "Why did you lie to me and Mama?"

Mary had been prepared for an answer but not for a question. She looked at Mama and said, "I'm sorry, Mrs. Harper, I did lie about that, but I only did it to protect Joshua. I was scared of that Jimmy Jones and his father."

"It's all right, Mary," Mama said. She turned to me. "If

you don't stop sassing Mary and answer her question, I'm going to . . ." But instead of finishing her sentence, Mama slowly lowered her head onto the table and started sobbing. Winifred leaned over and started whispering something to her.

After a few minutes Mama stopped sobbing and I started talking. I told them everything that had happened, from catching Joshua slipping downstairs to get something to eat because he thought I was asleep to our being chased by Klansmen when they discovered us watching them whip Theodore.

"But I'm sure Joshua really has gone to Chicago this time, Mary," I said, "and I know he'll telephone you as soon as he can too."

For what seemed like forever, both Mama and Mary just looked at me, but then Mama said, "Woodrow, I just don't understand how you can possibly feel anything for a man who would take a whip to another human being." She stood up and walked around to where Mary was sitting. She put her hand tentatively on Mary's shoulder, then bent down and hugged her. "You know yourself that's what Joshua wanted to do all along, Mary, ride a freight train to Chicago, so that's probably what he had in mind when those men were chasing him."

Mary sighed heavily. "I do hope and pray you're right,

Mrs. Harper. Joshua's a good boy, and he knows I worry about him." She placed her hands on the table to help her stand up. "I just need to have faith in the Good Lord that He's looking after him."

I watched Mary walk slowly back to the sink. She seemed to have aged several years in just the few minutes she had been sitting at the table with us. Mama sat back down and for several minutes the three of us looked at one another uncomfortably.

Finally I stood up. "I think I'll go to my room and read." How many times had I used that excuse over the years, I wondered, to get away from anything in my life that I couldn't deal with?

"I need to get home myself," Winifred said. "James will wonder what happened to me." She stood up too. "Will you be all right?" she asked Mama.

Mama nodded. "Thank you for all your help, Winifred. It means a lot to me. And I'm sorry I was so cross with you earlier."

Winifred leaned over and gave Mama a big hug.

I went on upstairs. Before I got to my room, I walked to the window at the end of the hallway to look at Senator Crawford's house, and that's when I saw Jimmy coming out the front door with a picnic basket in his hands. *What is he doing over there?* I wondered, suddenly jealous. He didn't need Senator Crawford the way I did. I went on into my room to read, but I couldn't get the image of Jimmy and the picnic basket out of my mind. Down the hall, I heard Mama's door close, so I guessed that Winifred had left and that Mama had locked herself away from the world. A heaviness was pressing down on me so hard that I could barely breathe, and I knew I had to find out what was going on next door. Senator Crawford's house had been the only place I felt safe, but now I wondered if it really was. Was that too going to be taken away from me?

I knocked several times, but no one answered. Just as I was about to leave, the door finally opened, and Senator Crawford was standing there unsteadily, his face bright red. I could smell on his breath that he had been drinking. "Woodrow," he said. My name came out of his mouth slurred and twisted and not pleasant sounding at all, and I didn't know what to think. Neither of us said anything for a couple of minutes, then Senator Crawford stepped aside and opened the door wider for me to come inside. "I've been enjoying some whiskey, some of the good stuff Brother Jones picks up along the Red River," he told me as he led me deeper into the house. "Some people call it 'white lightning,' and that's a really good name for it too, because I can see all these white lightning flashes in front of my eyes." He stopped and turned around to face me. In the dim light his face looked like a Halloween mask. "You'd better go back and shut the front door."

I did as he told me and then followed him into his study. He was already sitting at his desk, with three mason jars in front of him. He picked up one that was half full and drank from it, grimacing as he swallowed what was left. "Damn, that burns, but it's what I need, son, because hell is going to be a lot hotter than this stuff," he said. He gave me a crooked smile. "I'm just getting myself ready for the trip I'll have to take one of these days, boy, that's all."

"What do you mean?" I asked him.

He suddenly looked at me as though he were seeing me for the first time. "Nothing. Sit down, Woodrow, we need to talk."

I sat down in the chair in front of him. For several minutes, Senator Crawford just looked at me. He seemed to be having trouble focusing. Finally he managed to look straight into my eyes. "If I don't have a son to teach all the secrets, Woodrow, then I'll have to give up Robert's purple robe and hood to someone else, and I don't want to do that. I was destined to have a boy who would be the next imperial wizard, because my father and my grandfather were wizards, and I am a true believer in the superiority of the white race." He stopped and twisted off the lid of another mason jar and raised it to his mouth. I watched his Adam's apple bobbing up and down as he drank almost all of the white lightning. He put the jar down, let out his breath, and then wiped his mouth with his sleeve. "I had it all planned out so carefully." He let out a sob. "It wasn't my fault that Robert got himself killed in France." He suddenly switched to a different subject. "Jimmy's been helping me take care of another matter, something I don't want to talk about now," he continued. He took another drink from the mason jar. "Jimmy says he doesn't trust you. He doesn't think you're a true believer."

"I'm trying hard to believe, sir. I really am!"

"I know you are, Woodrow, but I'm going to have to give you a test just to make sure."

chapter FOURTEEN

*W*hy would someone who keeps telling me that I am like a son to him need to give me a test to prove my loyalty? I wondered. The thought really hurt me, but before I could tell Senator Crawford how I felt, his head hit the desk with a thud, knocking over the last mason jar. The white lightning spilled over the edge of the desk and started dripping onto the hardwood floor. After it finally stopped, all I heard was Senator Crawford's snoring.

"You'd better go home, Mr. Woodrow."

I turned and saw Benjamin standing in his bathrobe at the door of the study. "I need to stay with him," I said. Benjamin shook his head. My first reaction was to argue, because I wasn't going to let Senator Crawford's Negro tell me what to do, but something in Benjamin's eyes told me I should do as he asked. "All right," I said. I was barely out the front door before I heard Benjamin lock it behind me.

When I got to my house, there was enough moonlight coming in through the tall front windows that I didn't need to turn on a light to go upstairs. I didn't go to my room; instead, I headed for the attic. I had decided there was something I needed to do. Daddy was dead, but as long as his things were in this house, he was still a presence. And I didn't want a memory for a father; I wanted someone who wanted me for a son. *Senator Crawford*. From the first day we met, Senator Crawford understood me more than anyone else ever had, and he had made it clear how important I was to him. Seeing him so distraught tonight, hearing his longing for the son he'd lost, made me surer than ever that the man who wanted to take me fishing and teach me how to paint couldn't be an evil person. He was just angry because his wife and son were dead, and he was taking that anger out on other people. I needed Senator Crawford, and he certainly needed me. When Mama understood how I was going to change the Klan, then maybe she wouldn't hate it so much. And in time, maybe Mama would even learn to accept how important Senator Crawford was to me.

When I got to the attic, I pulled all of the clothes out of the trunk labeled 1880–1881 and took them downstairs. I got some matches from the kitchen, then I carried the clothes out to the alley and threw them into one of the huge oil drums that served as our garbage cans. I had to use five matches, but I finally got the clothes to burn and within just a few minutes they were reduced to ashes. I went back to the attic and emptied the next trunk, but when I got to the alley, two policemen were climbing out of their patrol wagon. "It's a little late to be burning trash, isn't it, son?" one of them said.

"I thought you could burn trash any time you wanted to," I told him.

"You can, but most people don't burn it this late at night," the second policeman said. "What are you getting rid of?"

"Clothes," I said.

The first policeman shined a flashlight onto the pile of clothes I was holding. "You shouldn't be burning those, son. I know a lot of people who can use them."

I shook my head. "I'm not giving them away. If I can't burn them, then nobody's getting them."

"You're a real smart-aleck, aren't you?" the first policeman said, "and selfish to boot."

"Senator Crawford doesn't think so."

The second policeman shined his flashlight into my eyes. "Do you know Senator Crawford?"

"I know him very well. He says I'm like a son to him."

"Well, that's actually why we're here, to find out why he's not at the parade. They sent us to get him. But we saw this fire, and we thought we'd better investigate that first."

"What parade?" I asked.

"The Klan is having a large torchlight parade through downtown Lawton tonight," the second policeman said. "Senator Crawford was supposed to lead it."

"Oh, *that* parade. Well, uh, he was planning to go," I said, realizing I couldn't let them know that the senator had passed out from white lightning, "but he has an upset stomach, something that nigra of his fixed for supper, and he was just trying to get it settled before he left."

The two policemen laughed. I had said the right words about Benjamin, so now everything was all right.

"I'm going to go check on him again after I finish here. Why don't you go back and tell the Klan to start the parade? If Senator Crawford gets to feeling better, he'll be there, and if he doesn't, they'll just have to have the parade without him. They all know what to do."

"You sound as though you know what to do too," the first

policemen said. He shined his flashlight again on the pile of clothes I still had in my arms. "Are you sure you have to burn those?" he asked.

"Yes, I am," I said.

I tossed the rest of the clothes into the fire, causing sparks to fly up into the air. Within a few minutes, the clothes began to smolder, and then they suddenly burst into flames. Without saying another word, the two policemen got back into the patrol wagon and drove on down the alley. I watched their taillights disappear. When the flames were no longer shooting past the rim of the barrel, I left to get more clothes, but before I reached the back door, I stopped and looked over at Senator Crawford's house. I knew there was no way Senator Crawford could lead a torchlight parade through downtown Lawton tonight, but maybe this was a chance for me to prove that he could trust me. Maybe I could pass my *own* test.

I knocked on the senator's door several times before Benjamin opened it. I could see by the look on his face that he wasn't planning to let me in, so I shoved right past him.

"Mr. Woodrow, I don't think you should be here."

"I have to get something, Benjamin." I hurried down the hall to Senator Crawford's bedroom. He wasn't there. I realized that Benjamin must have just left him where he was when I saw him last—passed out on his desk in the study. The thought made me angry.

"You need to leave here right now, Mr. Woodrow, before it's too late!" Benjamin's frame filled the doorway, and he didn't look like the same person who fulfilled Senator Crawford's every wish.

"I know what I'm doing, Benjamin." I went over to the wardrobe, pulled out the purple robe and hood that Senator Crawford had said were mine, and put them on.

"You can't take those. They belonged to Mr. Robert."

"Well, they belong to me now, and I'm going to wear them in the torchlight parade tonight."

"You can never replace Mr. Robert in the Senator's heart, Mr. Woodrow. He's just using you. He's—"

I whirled around. "You're wrong, Benjamin!" I shouted at him. "Senator Crawford treats me like a son!" I ran out of the house before Benjamin could say anything else. But as I walked toward the courthouse square, I couldn't help wondering about what he'd started to say. At times I stumbled on the uneven sidewalks and almost fell, but I managed not to, and when I finally reached the corner of Sixth Street and D Avenue, I saw that the Klansmen were beginning to line up on Fifth Street, on the other side of the square. I picked up my pace, and soon several of the Klansmen in white saw me and started applauding. I waved at them as I headed for the front of the parade column.

Some of the Klansmen carried huge banners that read: WE STAND FOR LAW AND ORDER! and KICK THE UNDESIRABLE ELEMENTS OUT OF TOWN! and STOP THE LAWLESSNESS NOW! There were no signs about hating Negroes, Catholics, or Jews.

Maybe it's going to be all right after all, I told myself.

When I reached the front, I saw a man in a red robe and hood. I assumed that he was one of the Klansmen who had helped Senator Crawford whip Theodore when Joshua and I had spied on the rally. I waved at him. He waved back and motioned me over. "Where's the senator?" he whispered.

"He's at home. He has a really bad stomachache," I whispered back. "He gave me Robert's robe and told me to lead the parade."

"Well, all right, then, if that's what he wants." He didn't sound too happy, but he probably knew better than to argue. "I'll get you a torch."

"Thank you," I said.

As the red Klansman turned to leave, I noticed a Klansman in a blue robe and hood standing a few feet away, staring at me. I was sure he was the other man who had helped Senator Crawford whip Theodore. Beside him there was someone my height dressed in a white robe and hood, and all of a sudden I knew I was looking at Jimmy and his father. I wondered if I should say something to them about Senator Crawford's being ill, but just then, the red Klansman returned with a torch, handed it to me, and said, "We can start the parade now."

I had no idea what I was supposed to do, but I lifted the torch high and started walking. As it turned out, it was easy, because all I had to do was follow the policemen in the patrol wagon who had come by to investigate the fire when I was burning Daddy's clothes. For that time of night, there were still quite a few people on the streets, and they cheered us as we marched past. When it was over, the red Klansman whispered, "Tell the senator I hope he gets to feeling better."

"I'll tell him," I said. I turned around and saw Jimmy and his father getting into their automobile. They didn't even look in my direction. All the other Klansmen were getting into their automobiles too, so I quickly started back the way I had come, and in a few minutes the darkness of the street had made me almost invisible.

chapter FIFTEEN

Early Monday morning I was awakened by Mama shouting, "What is this, Woodrow?"

"What is *what*, Mama?" I was rubbing my eyes, trying to focus on the object of her anger.

"Where did this purple robe and hood come from, and what are they doing in our house?"

"They're mine. Senator Crawford gave them to me."

"Well, I'm throwing them away!"

As she turned to leave, I jumped out of bed and grabbed the robe and hood from her. "No, you're not!"

Mama hadn't expected that, so they came easily out of her grasp. She quickly recovered, though, and tried to snatch them back from me, but I was too fast for her. For a few minutes we just stood and stared at each other. Finally Mama's face softened, and she said, "Woodrow, you're only thirteen years old. You don't know what you're doing."

"I know exactly what I'm doing, and it's going to work, too, if you would only just trust me."

Mama started toward me and I pulled back, but then I realized that she was only going to sit down on the side of my bed. "What is it exactly that you're going to do, Woodrow? I want to hear it from you so I'll understand."

"I'm just trying to survive, Mama. I'm just trying not to be an outsider anymore. Senator Crawford can help me. He *wants* to help me. He's not just a member of the Ku Klux Klan, he's the *imperial wizard of Oklahoma*. He wants me to become a leader of the Klan, like himself, and when I do, I'm going to change the bad things about the Klan. I keep telling you, Mama—I'm like a son to him, and he's like a father to me. He *listens* to me, and I know I can make him see how wrong some of the things the Klan does are."

Mama's breathing was becoming labored now, and her face was flushed. "Your *father* is dead, Woodrow. He died in an automobile accident back in Washington."

"I know that, Mama, but every day here I have to fight

to be accepted in this town, and his reputation doesn't help. I can't do this all by myself! People around here respect Senator Crawford, and they accept me because of him."

"I don't even know who you are anymore, Woodrow. You're not the same boy I came here with from Washington."

"I may not be, Mama, and I'm not comfortable with everything that's happening, but I really do think I've figured out how to make it better. I don't know how else to do it but this way."

"For all your father's faults, and there were many, Woodrow, the one thing he really couldn't stand when he was growing up was the way white people treated Negroes around here. He was never afraid to tell people how he felt about it, and some people called him a 'nigger lover,' but I'll tell you this, Woodrow, it made him proud when people said that about him."

When I didn't say anything, Mama stood up slowly and left the room. Downstairs, I heard the telephone ringing, and a couple of minutes later Mama stuck her head in and in an icy voice said, "It's your *friend* Jimmy Jones. He said he needs to talk to you. I started to hang up on him, Woodrow, but I've decided that you're the one who's going to have to sort this out for yourself."

I ran downstairs. "Hello!" I said.

"We're going to witness after school today, Woodrow, so don't make any other plans."

"I won't."

Mama was standing behind me when I hung up. "What did he want?"

"Nothing!" I went up to my room and dressed as quickly as I could for school.

Mama and I didn't speak to each other for the rest of the day. That afternoon, when we got home, I changed clothes and then sat out on the front porch to wait for Jimmy.

A few minutes later he rode up. "How do you like my bike?" he asked. "It just came this morning by Railway Express. It's a dual-suspension mountain bike and is actually made for the Italian army. It has telescoping seat stays, a leaf spring at the bottom bracket, a springer fork, and large-profile pneumatic tires."

I had no idea what Jimmy was talking about. "I just have a plain old Rover Safety."

"I actually think I'll be able to witness better on this bicycle, Woodrow. Are you ready?"

I nodded. "I'm ready!"

From my house, we headed north on Eighth Street until we reached Columbia. "There are lots of kids who live on this street who don't believe, Woodrow," Jimmy said. "They keep telling us to leave them alone, but we don't, and we never will, because Jesus Christ doesn't want us to."

I looked down both sides of the street. "I don't see anybody around."

Jimmy smiled. "Oh, they're there all right. We'll ride up and down this block and sooner or later some of them will come outside. That's when we'll yell things at them." With that, Jimmy raced toward the curb, jumped it, and started down the sidewalk at full speed.

There was no way I could catch up, I knew, but I walked my bicycle to the curb, lifted it up, climbed on, and started after him. I was only halfway down the block when he passed me going in the opposite direction. By the time I reached the corner, Jimmy was back with me. "Don't stop, Woodrow, and try to go faster!"

"All right," I said.

Jimmy took off again. I couldn't believe how fast his bicycle was. I tried to pedal faster, but the chain slipped, and for just a moment I thought I had stripped it, but then it caught, and I was on my way again. When I reached the middle of the block, I heard someone shout, "You'd better get out of here!" A boy about our age was standing in front of a gate looking directly at me. "You'd better get out of here!" he repeated. All of a sudden, none of the words that Jimmy said we'd yell at boys like this would form inside my mouth.

I heard Jimmy coming up behind me. He'd noticed the boy too and stopped to yell, "White trash! Nigger lover!"

"Get out of here!" the boy shouted back.

I pedaled on to the corner, but by the time I got there, Jimmy had already passed me and was halfway down the block again. I decided to wait at the corner for him to return.

Once again, when he got to the house where the boy was, he yelled, "White trash! Nigger lover!" before he continued on back toward me. "What's wrong?" he asked.

I shrugged.

"Why aren't you saying anything?"

"Because I just feel kind of dumb doing this, that's why," I surprised myself by saying.

Jimmy got off his bicycle and stood beside it. "Really?" The tone of his voice had turned icy. "Don't you believe in what the Klan is trying to do, Woodrow?"

"I do, but I don't see how yelling to that boy back there is helping the Klan."

"It's not just that boy, Woodrow. His grandfather is Leslie P. Ross, the founder of a group of people in Lawton who call themselves Constitutional Americans." He spat on the ground. "He's the most anti-Klan white person in this town, but I can tell you for sure that he and his family are scared to death of what we're going to do to them if they don't stop." Jimmy pointed across the street. I looked just as another boy ducked his head behind a gate. "That was Matthew Deaver. His father is the president of a bank, and he recently gave some niggers a loan to buy some farmland." He looked back at me. "We don't need any niggers owning land around here, Woodrow, acting like they're as good as white people."

"Why don't some of the Klansmen just *talk* to these men, Jimmy? If the Klan is right, wouldn't they be able to convince them not to do what they're doing?"

"Oh, they talked to them both, Woodrow, but they said they weren't afraid of us and that they weren't going to change their minds, so last week, one of the barns on Mr. Deaver's farm east of town caught fire and burned to the ground." He smiled. "Come on. We're going to another neighborhood."

Without waiting for me, Jimmy starting riding east on Columbia, but he wasn't going very fast, so it didn't take me long to catch up with him. We followed Columbia until we crossed some railroad tracks.

"Now we're in Niggertown," Jimmy said.

Before I could ask him why we had come here, since I had thought the whole point of what we were doing was to convince *white* kids to get their parents to support the Klan, he was already riding down the middle of the street. Finally Jimmy stopped in front of a small white-frame house with some pretty flowers in the yard but which could have used a paint job. He rode his bicycle right up to the porch.

I followed him. "Who lives here?" I asked.

Jimmy didn't answer me. Instead he started shouting, "Go back to Africa, niggers! Nobody wants you here!" After he had done this a couple of times, he stopped and looked at me. "What's the matter with you now, Woodrow?"

Just then the front door opened and a Negro man stepped out onto the porch. I could tell by his eyes that what he wanted to do was knock us off our bicycles, but that didn't stop Jimmy, who started shouting even louder. All of a sudden a woman appeared behind the man, and I saw that it was Mary.

Jimmy turned to me and smiled. I knew right away that this was the *witnessing* he had planned all along. He had already told Senator Crawford that he didn't trust me, and now *he* was testing me. *I'm not going to fail!* I told myself. *I'm not going to let him win!* I swallowed hard and took a deep breath. "Go back to Africa, niggers!" I screamed. "Nobody wants you here!" And I kept screaming it over and over and over, with tears streaming down my face, until Mary and the man, whom I guessed was her husband, finally stepped back inside the house and shut the door. I was still screaming it when I noticed that Jimmy was nowhere in sight. It took me several seconds to stop, because each time I tried, the words would still tumble out. It was almost like a train engine that had to slow down gradually before it could come to a complete halt. Finally, when there was nothing left inside my mouth, I leaned over the handlebars of the Rover Safety and vomited onto some of Mary's flowers.

I was trembling, but I knew that I couldn't stay there, because other Negroes had come out onto their front porches too and were staring at me. Somehow I managed to turn my bicycle around, and I pedaled out into the street and headed back west. I had no idea where I was, but I knew that all I had to do was stay on Columbia until I got to Eighth Street. By the time I crossed the railroad tracks, I had stopped trembling, but I couldn't get Mary's face out of my mind. Even when I shook my head from side to side, stupidly thinking that would help, her eyes stayed in front of me. I didn't know exactly why Jimmy had run off and left me. Had my screaming scared him? Or was he somehow angry that I had passed his test?

Finally I reached our street and pedaled to a stop in front of

Senator Crawford's house. I had to see him. Benjamin told me he was painting in the solarium, but his face didn't betray anything else. When I got back there, Senator Crawford finished a brush stroke before he looked up at me, but then he gave me a smile that told me everything was all right. "Sit, Woodrow," he said. "If you don't feel like painting, then we can just enjoy each other's company." I sat next to him on my stool as he gently added tiny veins to the orchid he was painting. As I watched his steady hand, I thought of a painting Mama had shown me once of the hand of God, and I felt as if this was like that hand, that Senator Crawford wasn't just painting this orchid, he was creating it, just as God had done. When he finished the vein, he turned to me and said, "Tell me everything." So I did, starting with the Klan parade the night before and ending with my shouting at Mary and her husband. "You did well, Woodrow," Senator Crawford said.

"Thank you, sir. Was any of that the *test* you were talking about?"

Senator Crawford started a second vein, but in the middle, he picked up his brush and turned to me again. "No, Woodrow, those were just things that happened to you." He smiled. "You'll be taking the test I was talking about around ten o'clock tonight."

chapter SIXTEEN

What will I have to do?" I finally asked, and right away knew that I must have been holding my breath a long time, because the question came out almost as a gasp.

Senator Crawford looked over at me and raised an eyebrow. "Now, Woodrow, it wouldn't be a test if I told you in advance, would it?"

"No, sir."

Senator Crawford sighed. "I'm sorry, Woodrow. I don't mean to be so ill-natured with you. I'm just a little shaky from last night, that's all."

"I was worried about you."

"And I appreciate that too. These last few days have been

difficult, for a lot of reasons, but all my questions should be answered tonight."

"I promise I'll be here."

When I opened our front door, I could hear Mama talking to Mary in the kitchen, and I was afraid Mary had told Mama what I had done earlier at her house. I wanted to escape to my room, but Mama heard me and called, "Woodrow? Would you come here, please?" She didn't sound angry, so maybe Mary hadn't said anything to her. "Did you enjoy your afternoon with Jimmy?" Mama took a sip of her coffee while she waited for my reply.

"Yes. We rode our bicycles all over town."

"That's nice. Mary will have dinner ready before long, so why don't you go ahead and wash up?"

"I'm not really hungry. I think I'll just go on to bed."

"Do as you please, Woodrow," Mama said coolly.

Mary had kept her back to us during the entire conversation. I was glad I didn't have to see her eyes on me again.

Mama took another sip of coffee. "Mary's staying here tonight. She has some things she wants to talk to me about. I'll see you in the morning."

I wanted to ask Mama what those "things" were, but I was sure I already knew. "All right," I said.

For the rest of the evening, I sat in my room and watched the clock. Finally, just before ten, I heard Mama's door close. I snuck downstairs and out the front door.

Senator Crawford was just backing the Buick Touring out of the garage. "Stop!" I shouted to him. I ran around to the other side and jumped into the front passenger seat. "Where are we going?"

"To my farm."

"I didn't know you had a farm. What do you grow on it?"

"Not too much anymore, Woodrow, because I don't have the time . . . or the energy, for that matter. But I have a man living in the house, and he keeps a few head of cattle, some chickens, and some goats."

At South Boundary Road, Senator Crawford turned east and drove a couple of miles before he turned south. Now we were on a dirt road, and dust was flying into the car. I rolled up the window on my side, but the dust didn't seem to bother Senator Crawford. His eyes were straight ahead. When he began to slow down, he looked at me and said, "We're here, Woodrow." He turned onto a narrower dirt road bordered by tall grass and weeds. It was almost like being inside a tunnel without a ceiling. The longer we drove down this road, the closer and taller the grasses and the weeds got, and soon I could smell the wildness of them. Finally we emerged into a clearing brilliantly lit by the full moon.

Up ahead, in the lights of the Buick Touring, I saw a small house, but Senator Crawford drove past it toward a barn several yards away. As we got closer, the headlights picked up another automobile parked by the barn, and I recognized it as Jimmy's father's. I turned to Senator Crawford and asked why Mr. Jones was here, but he continued to stare straight ahead. The barn doors swung open just as Senator Crawford turned off the engine. A tall man started walking toward us.

"That's Carl. He lives in the farmhouse back there." Senator Crawford and I got out of the automobile. I stood on the soft grass, waiting to be told what to do next. Senator Crawford and Carl were talking, but I couldn't hear what they were saying. After a while Carl nodded, gave me a quick glance, and headed off into the darkness toward the house. "Follow me, Woodrow," Senator Crawford called.

I joined him at the barn doors, and we went inside. I thought about a circus I had attended once in Baltimore with my parents. I never forgot that smell, which Mama had said was the hay they fed to the animals. I turned to tell Senator Crawford about it, but he was focused on something at the far corner of the barn where we were headed. There I could see a lightbulb hanging from a long electrical wire, and a Negro was standing in the center of the small circle of light it made. At the edge of the circle, almost in darkness, was Mr. Jones. And Jimmy was standing beside him.

Suddenly I stopped. "No!" I cried.

"Quiet!" Senator Crawford hissed. "Just be quiet!"

"That's Joshua," I whispered.

"Of course it is." Senator Crawford grabbed my arm and started pulling me along. "This is the test, Woodrow, and I expect you to pass it."

We were almost to the light before I realized Joshua was tied to a pole. There was a rope around his neck, a rope around his waist, and a rope around his ankles. His eyes were closed, and at first I was afraid he was dead, but then I saw his chest moving up and down.

"Is there a problem, Senator Crawford?" Mr. Jones asked.

"No, there's no problem," Senator Crawford replied. "There's no problem at all."

"Shall we begin the test then?" Mr. Jones said.

Senator Crawford nodded. Jimmy pulled a whip from behind his back, cracked it in front of him, and looked at me with a big grin. Mr. Jones stepped back, leaving Jimmy by himself just outside the circle of light. Jimmy gripped the handle of the whip, slowly raised it over his shoulder, and then, like lightning, struck out at Joshua. The cracking sound the whip made seemed to split the air around me, causing my ears to pop. My eyes were on Joshua's face when Jimmy's whip struck him, and I flinched at the same time Joshua flinched. Without even thinking, I started forward to help him, but Senator Crawford's grip on my arm was like a vise. "Don't move, Woodrow," he whispered into my ear.

I turned my eyes to Jimmy's face and forced myself to keep them there for the next four cracks of the whip. I could tell Jimmy was enjoying what he was doing. I hated myself for just standing there, doing nothing, and I wondered if that was the test—watching Jimmy whip Joshua, accepting that white people were allowed to do this to Negroes. But my palms were sweaty, and I knew that wasn't really the test.

Jimmy turned to me, gave me another big grin, and walked in our direction. When he reached the place where Senator Crawford and I were standing, he held out the whip and said, "Your turn, Woodrow."

"Take it, Woodrow," Senator Crawford said. "This is the test."

"You want me to whip Joshua too?" My voice was barely above a whisper.

Senator Crawford nodded. "If you're going to be the next imperial wizard, Woodrow, then you need to know how to whip niggers so they'll stay in line, because that's one of our main duties."

"Take it, Woodrow!" Jimmy shouted. My eyes locked onto his, and for the first time I saw that there was pure evil behind them. "Take it!" he shouted again. When I still hadn't moved after several more seconds, Jimmy tossed the whip at my feet and said, "You may have white skin, but you've got nigger blood inside you." Then he turned and walked back to his father. Senator Crawford followed him.

I was suddenly by myself. There was no air in the barn, and that sweet smell of hay that just moments before had brought back such wonderful memories of the circus suddenly stank of garbage. I closed my eyes to get away from it all. "Woodrow!" I heard my name being called, but it felt like a nightmare, not something that was really happening. "Woodrow!" The voice was louder this time, and I knew it was real. When I opened my eyes, I could see once again the pole in the small circle of light, with Joshua tied to it, and Senator Crawford, Jimmy, and his father standing just outside the light, waiting for me to lash Joshua's smooth black skin with the whip. "I can't!" I shouted at them. "I can't do it!"

Jimmy started laughing so loud that some pigeons roosting above us started flying wildly around the barn. "What would you expect from the son of a nigger lover? You're not worthy of that white skin you're inside."

"He's no better than his father," Mr. Jones said.

I could feel blood on my tongue from biting it so hard to keep from saying anything. How could I let Jimmy and his father talk about Daddy that way? *What would you have done if you were here instead of me, Daddy?* I wanted to shout. *I need your help!*

Senator Crawford was just staring at me. *And why did you have to be one of these people? Together we could have done so many of the things that I always wanted to do with Daddy!*

Mr. Jones turned to Senator Crawford and said, "Well, you have your answer now, don't you, Senator? Even you couldn't get the Klan to accept *him*. We're all going to meet in Medicine Park on Wednesday to talk about some changes in the leadership of the Klan. You just make sure you bring your own purple robe and hood and the ones you gave to this nigger-lovin' boy here." He turned to Jimmy. "Come on, son, we're leaving. This place is beginning to stink to high heaven!"

Jimmy giggled.

I looked back over at Senator Crawford, expecting now

to see him staring at me angrily, but he wasn't. What I saw in his face at that moment was what I had seen many times in Daddy's face, disappointment that I wasn't the son he really wanted. Daddy was dead, and if I disappointed Senator Crawford the way I had disappointed my father, I would have no one. I remembered how the senator had poured out his soul to me the night before; I just couldn't turn my back on him now. Just as Jimmy and his father reached the barn doors, I yelled, "I'll do it!"

They stopped and stared at me with what was almost disbelief on their faces. "It's too late, Woodrow!" Jimmy snarled.

"It is *not* too late!" I shouted at him. "It's never too late for the next imperial wizard of the Ku Klux Klan of Oklahoma to do anything!" Before either one of them could react, I headed toward the circle of light, clutching the whip tightly. My head was spinning, and my hands were shaking so hard, I was sure I would drop the whip.

When I reached the spot where Jimmy had stood just a few minutes ago, I stopped, took a deep breath, and flung the whip at Joshua's chest. Its crack seemed to split the air even more than it had before, and it drowned out the sob that had escaped from my throat.

Just like at Mary's house, I couldn't stop. I struck Joshua's chest four more times before I came to my senses. I couldn't look anyone in the eyes; all I could see was the blood covering Joshua's chest from the wounds Jimmy and I had made.

In a few minutes I heard an automobile start up outside, and I knew that Jimmy and his father were leaving. I hurried over to Senator Crawford, who hadn't moved from where he had been standing while I was whipping Joshua. When he finally turned to look at me, tears were streaming down his face. He reached out with both hands and placed them on my shoulders. "I knew right from the moment I saw you, Woodrow, that God had sent you to me." His chest suddenly shuddered as he took a deep breath. "He took away Robert, *but He sent you*, and now you've proven that you have the right to wear Robert's purple robe and hood and take your place alongside me, the imperial wizard of the Ku Klux Klan." Senator Crawford embraced me and held me tightly against his chest. "I am so sorry that I doubted you, Woodrow," he said, sobbing. "I am so sorry, and I promise you that I shall never doubt you again."

I had waited for what seemed like forever to hear these words from Senator Crawford, but all I could think about now was how he suddenly smelled like rotting meat. I pulled away. "We have to get Joshua to a doctor. Help me untie him."

Senator Crawford's eyes suddenly lost their focus. "We can't do that, son."

"But we have to! I did what you wanted me to, I whipped him, I passed the test, but now we need to make sure he's all right."

Senator Crawford began shaking his head. "No! No, no, no!" he shouted. "There would be questions, Woodrow. No, no, no, we can't do it!"

"Mary is very worried about him, Senator Crawford. She thinks he went to Chicago to stay with an uncle, and she doesn't understand why she hasn't heard from him." I was starting to panic. "He's been punished, just like you punished Theodore. Even if you won't take him to a doctor, we have to let him go so he can get help."

"No, Woodrow! There are just some niggers we can't let grow up because they'll always be a problem for us. Joshua has been trouble all of his life. He's rotten inside." He seemed to be getting more and more agitated. "If Mary was really honest with herself, she'd tell you that she wishes Joshua had never been born, because he's been such a burden to her. No, no, no! We're never going to let him go!"

"What do you mean? You can't keep him here forever."

"You're right, Woodrow, we can't," Senator Crawford said

with a twisted grin. "In fact, I don't really think he was ever here. After we chased him away from the Klan rally that you and he attended, he hopped a freight train to Chicago, and that's where he probably is right now." He shrugged. "You know how these young nigger bucks are. They're always fighting over one thing or another, and it wouldn't surprise me if Joshua didn't get this throat slit and if somebody hadn't tied some weights around him and dumped him into Lake Michigan."

I couldn't believe what I was hearing. "You can't just leave him here to die—that would be *murder* . . ." I stopped. The grin on Senator Crawford's face was wider now, and his teeth were showing. I had never before noticed how stained with yellow they were.

"It's not murder," Senator Crawford said. "It's not murder to kill an *animal*."

"I'm sorry for being so stupid, Daddy," I whispered.

"You don't have to be sorry, Woodrow. I still love you, and I'm going to help—"

I spat in his face. "I wasn't talking to you!" I screamed at him. "I was talking to my real father! I was apologizing to him for being too stupid to see how evil you were! All this talk about trying to clean up the lawlessness in Lawton is just to cover up what you really do, isn't it?"

The smile disappeared from Senator Crawford's face. He held out his hand. "Give me the whip!"

"No," I said, trying to keep my voice steady. "I'm not going to let you touch Joshua again."

I could see that it was taking a minute for my words to register, but then Senator Crawford's face turned red and the veins on the side of his neck started throbbing. "Hand it to me, Woodrow!"

Suddenly I heard such a loud rumble inside my head that I thought it was going to explode. Instead of handing Senator Crawford the whip, I raised it over my head and brought it back down with all the force I could muster and struck him in the face. I saw the shock in his eyes just seconds before he screamed. He grabbed his face and fell to the ground. He lay there, not moving, and I couldn't believe what I had just done.

"Woodrow." I turned and looked toward Joshua. He was straining to break the cords that held him. His chest was covered in bloody perspiration that reflected the dim light of the bulb. "Help me."

I looked around frantically for something with which to cut the cords that held him to the stake. Finally I saw a long scythe among some old-fashioned-looking farm implements piled in a corner of the barn. The blade was a little rusty, but I hoped it would be sharp enough to do the job. I grabbed it and hurried back over to Joshua. It felt like it took forever to cut through his bonds. When he was free, Joshua crumpled slowly to the hay. "I need some water, Woodrow," he said hoarsely. "It's in my room."

At first I thought Joshua must have been hallucinating, but then I noticed a door at the back of the barn, leading to a little room. It was really just a storage shed, but in the corner was a pallet, and next to the pallet was a straw picnic basket, which I realized was the one I'd seen Jimmy carrying out of Senator Crawford's house. I found a jug of water and took it to Joshua, all the time repeating, "I'm sorry, Joshua. I'm so sorry."

Senator Crawford still lay on the ground, but now he was moaning softly. "We have to get out of here," I told Joshua, "but I don't think I can find my way back to town."

"This is the same farm where the Klan rally was held, Woodrow, so all we have to do is follow Squaw Creek, but we need to hurry before Carl finds out what happened."

I had forgotten about Senator Crawford's farmhand. "Can you make it that far?"

"You'll have to help me a little, Woodrow, but I can make it. And this time I'm leaving Lawton for good."

"You're still bleeding, Joshua. We need to go to my house

first so Mama can put something on your wounds, and then we can talk about what to do next."

"No, I have to—," Joshua started to say, but I interrupted him with "You also have to see your mother, because she's been very worried about you."

"All right, then, let's go."

With each step toward the door, Joshua seemed to gain strength, and as we left the barn and headed toward Squaw Creek, he had to lean on me less and less. Within minutes we were at the barbed-wire fence and crawling under it.

"We're home free now, Woodrow, because I know every inch of the land from here back into Lawton."

Joshua took the lead, and I followed. He was weak, he told me, because no one had brought him any food for the last couple of days. Obviously, the Klan didn't want him in any condition to fight when Jimmy and I whipped him. The wounds from the lashing still stung, he said, but knowing that he was free kept him from thinking about it too much.

We rushed along at a pace that got us into town almost before I realized it, and Joshua knew exactly which yard to cut through to find our way to my street. We heard dogs barking in the distance, but none of them sounded close enough to be after us. Finally we reached I Avenue. Once we were on the street, we had to duck behind trees whenever we heard a car roaring by. When we got to my house, I was relieved to see that Senator Crawford's Buick Touring wasn't in his garage. I knew we had at least some time to get Joshua cleaned up and for him to say good-bye to his mother before finding a freight train to take him from Lawton to Chicago.

When Mary opened the front door, her mouth formed a scream, but I quickly pushed Joshua inside and slammed the door before it came out.

Mama rushed into the living room. "What's wrong?" she cried. When she saw Joshua, she said, "Get him upstairs to your room, Woodrow, and take off his clothes." She turned to Mary. "Go boil some water and bring up some towels."

"I'm all right," Joshua said.

Hearing him finally speak actually broke the tension in the room. "You're not all right, Joshua," I said. "You may be better than I first feared, but you're not all right."

Out of the corner of one eye, I saw Mama give me a questioning look, but I put my arm around Joshua's back and guided him upstairs and laid him on my bed.

Mama and Mary rushed into the room a few minutes later. Just as Mary started bathing the wounds, I stepped out of my room and into the dark hallway. I wondered if Joshua would tell them what had happened, that I was responsible for some of the welts on his chest. I knew I'd have to tell them all about it later, but right now I didn't want to think about it. I just wanted to close my eyes and escape from where I was. I walked over to the window, wondering if Carl had somehow gotten Senator Crawford home while I had been helping Joshua, and that's when I saw them. There was a long column of white-robed-and-hooded Klansmen, all holding torches, and they were walking slowly toward our house.

chapter SEVENTEEN

I raced downstairs and looked out one of the windows by the front door. The line of Klansmen stretched as far as I could see, and now I was certain we were surrounded. They were chanting something, but I couldn't make out what it was. I pulled aside the curtain just a little and put my ear to the window, but I still couldn't understand the words.

"Woodrow?" I turned and looked up to see Mama standing at the top of the stairs. "Why?"

"I used a whip on Senator Crawford, because he made me use it on Joshua."

For just a moment, I wasn't quite sure how Mama was

going to respond to my confession, but finally she said, "We can't let them win, Woodrow! We can't."

"I know that now, Mama."

When I looked out the window again, the Klansmen were almost to the edge of our property, and now I could understand what they were saying. *We want the nigger and the nigger lover. We want the nigger and the nigger lover."* All of a sudden I knew what to do. I picked up the phone and told the operator, "Leslie P. Ross, please."

A woman answered on the third ring. I explained what was happening and told her we needed Mr. Ross to help us. I hung up, hoping he would be able to. When I got back to the living room, Mary had joined Mama on the landing, and the two of them were standing close together with their arms around each other. Just then the inside of our house was lit by bright orange flickers. I rushed to the window and saw an enormous cross burning on the front lawn. Next to the cross stood two Klansmen, a father and son, dressed in what looked like brand-new purple robes and hoods, and I knew that Jimmy and his father finally had what they had always dreamed of—control of the Ku Klux Klan in Lawton. But for Jimmy there remained one other matter to deal with, me, because to him I was a traitor to all white people. I could see him bending the whip he was holding in his hand back and forth, not taking his eyes off the front door of our house.

"What are we going to do, Woodrow?" Mama called down to me in a strong voice.

"I'll take care of it, Mama. I'll do what Daddy would have done."

I remembered how when we arrived in Lawton, I had seen that soldier wink at Mama and had wondered then if I should have done something about it. I knew now what was going to happen next was all up to me. Daddy would expect me to take care of her. The Klansmen surrounding our house couldn't know for sure that Joshua was in our house. If I went out and faced them and told them that Joshua wasn't here, Jimmy might whip me, but that might just be enough time for Mama, Mary, and Joshua to escape. "In just a few minutes, all the Klansmen will be gathering in our front yard," I told Mama and Mary. "When that happens, I want you to take Joshua out the back door, down the alley, and over to Winifred's house." I gripped the handle of the front door and turned the knob.

"Woodrow!" Mama screamed.

"It's all right, Mama. Now, please just do what I said!" I had the door half open, and I knew that some of the Klansmen must have noticed, because the chanting had stopped.

Finally the door was open all the way, and I was standing there framed in it as the light from the burning cross turned my skin yellow.

"Woodrow Harper!" Jimmy shouted, brandishing his whip. "Come forward to take your punishment, nigger lover!"

I took a deep breath and stepped out onto the front porch. The only sound was the crackling of the burning cross. I walked slowly toward the steps. Just as I reached them, though, I noticed that several of the Klansmen had broken rank and were pointing toward the street in front of our house. I looked and saw what appeared to be hundreds of people, Negroes and whites, holding hands and walking toward the circle of Klansmen, making their own circle around them. When they were just a few feet away, they stopped, and a man with a megaphone stepped forward. "I am Leslie P. Ross, and I am the chairman of a group called Constitutional Americans, and we have one goal: to drive the Ku Klux Klan not only out of Lawton and Comanche County but out of the entire state of Oklahoma." The people holding hands cheered. "You Klansmen may think your identities are hidden behind those robes and hoods, but people talk, and we know who all of you are!"

"Go home! Go home!" the crowd began to shout angrily. "Go home! Go home!"

I stood there and watched as the circle of Klansmen, clearly outnumbered, began to disintegrate. The people standing behind them moved apart just enough to let Klansmen pass through so they could get to their automobiles. For several minutes everyone just looked around in wonderment, not believing that they had actually stood up to the Ku Klux Klan.

Mr. Ross started walking toward our porch. When he reached the bottom step, he said, "Are you Woodrow Harper?"

I nodded. "Yes, sir." Mr. Ross held out his hand, and I went down the steps and shook it. "I'm sorry about what happened at your house this afternoon—"

Mr. Ross put up his hand to stop me. "You did a brave thing tonight, and you should be proud of yourself. But you need to know that these people who want to spread their hatred won't go away quietly." He shook my hand again. "I'm sure I'll be seeing you around town, Woodrow, and I hope you'll join us in helping to defeat the Ku Klux Klan."

"I'll do what I can, sir." I stood on the porch and watched the people disappear into the night, just as they had appeared, and then I turned to look next door at Senator Crawford's house. There were still no lights on. I didn't know if he was there, maybe even looking out a window at me, but I did know that I no longer cared. I went back inside and saw Mama and Mary standing just a few feet away.

"Are you all right?" Mama asked.

"Yes," I said.

"I called Winifred and she called Dr. Massey. He's coming over to examine Joshua."

"Is he okay?"

"I think so, but Mary just wants to be sure before we . . ." She stopped.

"Before we *what?*"

"We need to talk about what we're going to do now, Woodrow."

We talked late into the night—Mama, Mary, Joshua, and I. I realized that the Klan had actually done us a favor, because it had shaken Mama out of her depression. I knew it would take me a long time, maybe forever, to forgive myself for some of the things I'd done in Lawton, but I had finally discovered something I shared with my father.

In the end we decided to sell the house and move back to Washington. That was what Mary had wanted to talk to Mama about—her and Joshua's eventually going back East with us— not what Jimmy and I had done at her house. Of course, they both still thought then that Joshua was somewhere in Chicago.

At first Joshua was against the whole plan, but I figured it was only because he had grown to be against anything white people wanted him to do. He finally grudgingly acknowledged that it was white people joining with Negroes who had stopped the Klan from burning down our house.

Outside I heard a noise. I pulled back the curtains of one of the front windows. The wooden cross had collapsed, and now there were just scattered embers on our lawn. Two men walked up with metal buckets and threw water on the embers. White smoke rose from the charcoal, then slowly dissipated. Finally all of the embers were out, and the two men left.

I turned and started up the stairs. "I'm not really sleepy. I think I'll start packing now."

EPILOGUE

Two weeks later, the four of us—Mama, Mary, Joshua, and I—boarded a train that would take us from Lawton to Washington, D.C., after connections in Oklahoma City and St. Louis.

Mama and I had a comfortable Pullman compartment all the way, but Mary and Joshua only had coach seats in the one crowded car reserved for Negroes, and Joshua's seat was broken.

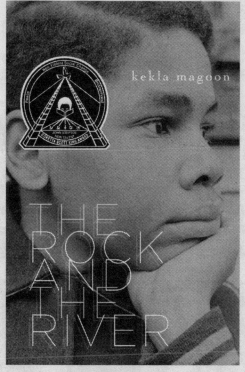

The Childhood of Famous Americans series: Books for Black History Month

Inspiring
people,
inspiring
stories

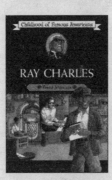

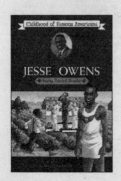

From Aladdin · Published by Simon & Schuster